"We thought you were Gryx the Terrible," Hercules said. Perhaps they could find out more about this tyrant ... and the "day of choosing" that the barkeeper had mentioned.

"No, he does not live here."

"Young Morvé said your village paid tribute to him."

"Oh?" Oram frowned. "The young are often confused by such things. It is not tribute—we pay for his protection."

"Who is he?" The old man hesitated as if trying to decide how to explain a very complicated matter.

Suddenly a loud crashing noise came from outside. Hercules sprang from his seat. It sounded like something large had fallen. He glanced at the others, then rushed to the door. Atalanta followed on his heels.

Hercules spotted movement in the mouth of a cave about halfway up the mountain. Slowly, as he watched, a creature emerged. Roughly man-shaped, it would have towered over the tallest human who ever lived. It had to be more than twenty feet tall, he thought, and it had knotted arms like tree trunks, a huge barrel chest, and long, thick legs. Its face looked vaguely human, but lumpy, as if half formed from clay. A thick black shag of beard grew around its mouth, and its hair hung down in ratty knots.

But what drew Hercules' gaze was the one huge eye set in the middle of its forehead. Slowly the creature blinked, then threw back its head and roared. The sound carried even to where they stood.

"That," Uram said heavily, "is Gryx."

Other Hercules adventures
from Tom Doherty Associates

THE WRATH OF POSEIDON
THE VENGEANCE OF HERA
THE GATES OF HADES*

*forthcoming

HERCULES
The Vengeance of Hera

John Gregory Betancourt

TOR *fantasy* ®

A TOM DOHERTY ASSOCIATES BOOK
NEW YORK

This is a work of fiction. All the characters and events portrayed in this book are either products of the author's imagination or are used fictitiously.

HERCULES: THE VENGEANCE OF HERA

Copyright © 1997 by John Gregory Betancourt

Cover art by Latif Kazbekov

A Tor Book
Published by Tom Doherty Associates, Inc.
175 Fifth Avenue
New York, NY 10010

Tor Books on the World Wide Web:
http://www.tor.com

Tor® is a registered trademark of Tom Doherty Associates, Inc.

ISBN: 0-812-53911-7

First edition: September 1997

Printed in the United States of America

0 9 8 7 6 5 4 3 2 1

ONE

RAIN POUNDED, THUNDER ROARED, and flashes of lightning cut crooked paths across the night sky. In the stern of the great sailing ship *Argo*, Hercules clung to the rudder's steering bar as rivers of water poured from his hair and beard. He squinted up into the darkness just as a new sheet of rain half blinded him. He brushed it from his eyes with the back of one hand. By the gods, he had never seen such a storm as this.

It had come upon them two days out from Troy. The speed and ferocity of its wind, driving them out to sea and far off course, made him suspect magic . . . the foulest sorcery of Hera, Queen of the Gods, or perhaps of Poseidon, who ruled the seas. Hera had always persecuted him. Thinking back, he remembered how rudely he had entered her temple in Troy when he and his friends had ventured into the catacombs beneath that city to slay a huge serpent there. She might easily have taken offense, he realized. Or Poseidon might be punishing them for killing the sea-monster he had sent to tear down Troy's walls. Either way, it offered no help. Hercules sighed and gave a little shrug; lately the gods seemed to take offense at whatever he did, whether he meant insult or not.

Hunching his shoulders against the rain and driving wind, he held the rudder more strongly. The rolling waves threatened to wrench control of the ship from him, but he used every ounce of his strength to keep the *Argo* headed bow-first into the waves. Jason, captain of the ship and leader of their quest for the Golden Fleece, had told him the *Argo* might capsize if he didn't.

It would be just like Hera to kill all the Argonauts simply to get to him, he thought. What did she care if their quest succeeded or failed, as long as she got her way? He raised his head defiantly, glaring up at the heavens.

"It won't work!" he shouted. The wind seemed to suck his words away. "This is just a storm, and we can sail through it!"

A huge wave broke over the bow, sending a sudden flood rushing toward him. The few men still working on deck clung desperately to the mast and railings until the water began to subside. Then, with its deck clear for the moment, the *Argo* began a long, slow slide into the trough between waves, starting the process over again.

Feeling like a half-drowned rat as the water drained from the deck around him, Hercules tightened his grip on the rudder. Had he ever been this wet before? He didn't think so, not even when he had shifted the course of the Alpheus and Peneus rivers to clean the Augean Stables. The lionskin he always wore felt like a lead weight from all the water it had soaked up.

"I won't give in!" he shouted again. Glaring defiantly at the sky, he pulled himself up straight. He would not give the god or goddess responsible the satisfaction of knowing he or she had made him uncomfortable.

Around the ship, wind howled like a pack of wolves,

and lightning flickered again. The rain battered down stronger than ever, but he no longer tried to shield himself from it; he couldn't be any wetter. Instead, he threw back his head and roared his defiance.

"You can't beat me, Hera!" he cried, and then he laughed. "It *is* you, isn't it?"

As if in reply, a mountain of water rose before the *Argo*. The ship creaked alarmingly as this wave—the largest yet—crashed across the bow, completely submerging the deck. Hercules felt a deep shudder run through the ship as she sought to turn. Not today, he thought grimly. Muscles straining, with water up to his chest, he held the rudder steady and kept the ship's bow pointed into the storm.

Slowly the water began to recede: waist deep, then knee deep, then ankle deep, then gone. Fortunately, none of the crew had been swept overboard, he saw with relief.

"*Hercules!*" a distant voice shouted. "I saw—"

A sudden gale swept the rest of the words away.

Raising his head, Hercules peered forward into the driving rain. Who had called his name? Jason? He could barely see ten paces ahead in the gloom. Keeping one hand on the rudder, he raised his other to shield his eyes. Lightning flickered, revealing a few dark forms huddled near the mast; they seemed to be trying to do something with the rigging.

"*Hercules!*" the voice called again. "*Lights ahead! I saw lights—*"

This time, Hercules recognized the deep-timbered voice of his friend and captain, Jason. Jason was pulling himself along the ship's railing toward him. Hercules frowned; that definitely meant trouble. Jason was supposed to be lashed in the bow watching for rocks—a storm such as this could run them aground with only a few seconds' warning, splintering the ship's hull like kindling. What kind of lights could Jason have seen? Were they approaching land . . . or another ship?

"Turn us!" Jason shouted. "Hercules—we're going to run aground!"

Hercules leaned on the rudder with all his strength. Slowly the ship began to veer to the right—*starboard*, he had to remind himself. He was not a sailor and was only now getting used to the ways of the sea. They couldn't afford to hit anything out here. In this storm, the crew wouldn't stand a chance of swimming ashore.

Jason reached him. He looked even wetter than Hercules felt, if that was possible.

"What is it?" Hercules shouted over the storm. "The mainland?"

"I think it's an island!" Jason shouted back. "We'll have to go around it!"

"How big? Can we make it into a harbor?"

"It's too risky in this weather! We don't know if there are rocks or shoals!"

Hercules gave a nod. Jason was right, of course. They couldn't afford the chance. He continued to lean on the rudder, and the great ship came around on her new course.

Jason began to make his way forward again, holding on to the railing and ducking his head into the slashing rain. In another burst of lightning, Hercules saw a huge wave rising up to their port side. Now that the *Argo* had turned, this one would break across the middle of the ship, he saw with rising panic.

"Jason!" he screamed. "Watch out—!"

The wave smashed over the deck, burying everyone and everything. Hercules saw Jason clutch the railing with both hands, but then water covered him. A second later, when the wave began to recede, he was gone. The railing stood empty.

Hercules blinked, and the reality of the situation hit him. Jason had been washed overboard.

TWO

"JASON!" HERCULES SHOUTED, QUICKLY lashing the rudder down with the ropes they tied there earlier in the storm, in case anything like this happened. He ran to where he had last seen his friend.

Several other crewmen had seen Jason vanish, too. They joined Hercules at the railing, staring down into the dark, churning water below. It was impossible to see anything. Where had he gone?

"Help!" a faint voice called from the waves. "I'm over here! Hercules!"

A new tongue of lightning flickered overhead, and Hercules spotted Jason's head bobbing in the water about fifty feet out from the ship. The waves seemed to be carrying him away rapidly. In this storm, the men wouldn't have much time to rescue Jason, Hercules knew. By the time they brought the ship around, he would be long gone.

"Find a rope," he told the man next to him—Orpheus, he saw.

"I already have one." Orpheus hefted the coil he held. Hercules estimated it at a hundred feet. "Do you think you can throw it far enough to reach him?" Orpheus asked.

"No," Hercules said. He threw off his lionskin. "I'll have to swim out to him. It's the only way." He knew none of the others would have a chance.

Faintly, Jason's voice reached them again: *"Help— Hercules—help!"*

"Hold on!" Hercules shouted. Quickly he knotted one end of the rope around his chest while Orpheus tied the other end to the railing. Then, naked except for the rope, he dove over the side of the *Argo*.

The sea rushed up and covered him, so cold it felt like a slap in the face. Kicking, pulling himself through the water in the direction he'd last seen Jason, he could hear his heart pounding in his ears. At last his lungs began to burn. He knew he couldn't go any farther without air.

Breaking the surface, he gulped in deep breaths and tried to get his bearings. Rain splashed everywhere, half blinding him. Waves broke around him. Wind roared in his ears.

Treading water, he turned until he had the dark, looming shape of the *Argo* behind him. That meant Jason had to lie straight ahead.

Tucking his head down, he began to swim strongly toward where he thought he'd seen his friend. Luckily, the current seemed to be pulling him forward, and he thought he was making good speed. Hopefully, he could reach Jason before he ran out of rope.

Every so often he glanced back at the *Argo* to maintain his bearings. The ship seemed to be drawing away with alarming speed. If he didn't find Jason soon, he knew he never would. He had only a hundred feet of rope. Would it be enough?

"Where are you?" he shouted. "Jason! Answer me! Jason? *Jason?*"

"Here—" came a weak reply to his left. "Over here—"

Hercules struck out in that direction. Waves surged around him. As he began to tire, he felt the rope start to drag him down. Rain filled his mouth and nose whenever he turned his head to draw a breath. Even so, he did not hesitate. He knew he was Jason's only hope.

Then, when he reached the crest of a wave, he suddenly saw a dark shape a few feet ahead. Jason—it had to be Jason.

He reached for his friend, and abruptly the rope stopped him. He pulled, but it didn't move at inch farther. He'd reached its end, he realized with frustration: it was too short. Quickly he pulled it down and looped it around his right ankle. Then, stretching out as far as he could, he reached for Jason—and found himself a few inches too short.

"Behind you, Jason!" he called, but the wind howled like a wild beast, catching his words and taking them away. He didn't think his friend had heard him, and the waves began to carry him away again. Curse his luck— would he get so close only to lose Jason now? For a second he thought of letting go of the rope and swimming after Jason, but he knew that would be suicide. He'd never make it back to the *Argo* with Jason.

"*Jason!*" he screamed. "*Turn around! Jason!*"

Slowly Jason splashed around. Hercules saw his friend's eyes widen in surprise and recognition.

"Swim to me!" Hercules called, reaching out as far as he could. "I can't go any farther—I'm tied to the ship!"

Feebly, Jason swam toward him. The second Hercules felt fingers touch his own, he seized Jason and pulled him close. Jason's head vanished under the water for a second, but Hercules had him and wasn't about to let go. Using all his strength, he managed to lift Jason's head above the waves.

The rope around his ankle suddenly went tight. Hercules felt himself being pulled through the water toward the *Argo* as Orpheus and the others hauled the rope in. He rolled onto his back, careful to keep his grip on Jason. He hadn't come this far to lose him now.

The trip back seemed to take an eternity. Hercules' arms and back began to ache from the strain, and his vision blurred from the rain. Even so, he managed to flip around and help pull himself up the last few feet, holding a now-limp Jason over one shoulder.

The men on deck eased them both over the railing. Hercules collapsed onto his back, gasping. He'd never felt so wet in all his life, he thought, forcing a laugh. He'd done it. He'd saved Jason.

"Is he—?" Orpheus asked.

"Quite alive, thanks to Hercules!" Theseus cried after a quick check. "We'll get him to his cabin and—"

Water sluiced over them as another huge wave broke across the deck. Hercules felt the sea pulling at him, dragging him across the deck. He tried to grab hold of something to keep from being swept overboard, but his hands came up empty—and then he felt wood slam against his back as the water shoved him against the railing. That was better than being swept overboard, he realized. Not that he could have gone far with the rope still around his ankle. But what about Jason and the others?

A moment later the water began to recede. Pulling himself to his feet, Hercules found everyone still on deck, clinging to ropes and each other. At least they had been spared this time. As he watched, Theseus and Orpheus threw Jason's arms over their shoulders and started aft for his cabin. Hercules gave them an approving nod. They would see to Jason better than he could. Orpheus had some knowledge of the healing arts; he would see to whatever injuries Jason might have suffered.

He glanced around for his lionskin. He had worn it so many years, he felt odd without it now. Had it washed overboard? No—Hylas had lashed it securely around the mast. Hercules untied it and shrugged it on. It was full of water and weighted him down like a stone, but it was almost a part of him. It would dry soon enough, given half a chance.

Then Hercules looked back toward the rudder. It had broken free of its lashings, leaving the *Argo* drifting at the mercy of wind and waves. Panic surged through him as he remembered the lights that Jason had seen ahead. Their course! If it took them toward that island again—

Turning, he scrambled for the rudder. Before he made it ten feet, though, the deck underfoot jolted to a shuddering stop and a horrible scraping sound filled the air. Everything started to slide toward the prow of the *Argo*.

Caught off balance, Hercules pitched forward and went skidding up the deck, eyes wide with sudden terror.

THREE

WITTA SMOOTHED HER SIMPLE gray robes, then knelt before the altar in the Temple of Athena. Outside, storm winds howled as thunder cracked and rumbled. The driving rain hissed as it fell. It had to be midnight, she thought; the time had come to make her offering to the goddess Athena.

As if sensing her decision, the young white goat tied on the offering stone began to bleat in rising panic.

"Easy." Witta stroked the animal's head with one gnarled old hand. With her other hand, she picked up the bronze sacrificial dagger lying at her side. "Easy."

Trembling, the goat grew still. Its eyes, wide and black, stared into her own. Witta felt a pang of sympathy, but she knew this had to be done, and done properly, for the good of her people. She sacrificed a goat every time Gryx spoke from the mountain. He would be coming tomorrow, and he always demanded a terrible tribute.

"I offer this beast to Pallas Athena, who watches over this land and these people," she cried in a singsong voice. "May she look after us and bless us in our time of need."

In one quick motion she slit the goat's throat, and as dark blood gushed forth, she caught it in a broad red bowl painted with black line drawings of owls and olive trees. The goat's dying eyes shone yellow in the lamplight. Then they turned gray.

"Witta," the goat said with a woman's voice.

Witta jumped, startled and alarmed. Magic—it had to be! She threw herself to the floor, prostrating herself before the altar. The goddess had never spoken to her before. She didn't know what else to do.

"Witta," the goat said again. "You have long been a good and faithful servant. As your reward, I will bring a ship to Thorna. Sail on it. Thus will your people be saved."

"Great goddess," Witta said hesitantly. "How will they be saved? What must I do?"

"You will know when the time comes."

"But *how*?"

There came no answer. Slowly, Witta raised her head. She found only the goat, now quite dead, its lifeless eyes fixed on distant fields she could not see. The goddess had gone.

Shivering, Witta rose and covered the goat with a white cloth. She could scarcely believe what had happened. The goddess had spoken to her. To *her*. She felt like laughing and dancing and singing in joy. The goddess would save them. It was the answer to all her prayers.

She set the bowl of blood on the altar stone and picked up the goat's body. Normally she would have given the goat to those in the village who needed its meat, but it had been touched by the goddess herself. She would skin it and make an offering basket from its hide. Its carcass would be buried beneath the altar, to keep the temple holy.

Outside, the rain continued to pound as thunder rumbled. Strong winds shook the walls of the temple, and dust sifted down from the rafters, where small white owls perched and watched with wide-open eyes.

What sort of ship would it be? Once a year, always in the early spring, traders from Syria visited the island. They had come and gone three months before. Did that mean the Syrians would return . . . or would strangers be on the ship?

Witta bowed her head. It didn't really matter. As long as the journey would save her people, she would undertake it.

FOUR

SLOWLY, HARDLY DARING TO breathe, Hercules picked himself up. He felt dizzy and disoriented, but he didn't seem to be hurt. He paused for a heartbeat, listening over the sounds of the storm and the sea. He no longer heard the soft creaking of the *Argo*'s timbers, just the sharp crack of sails and the slapping sound of waves against the hull. Something felt wrong.

Suddenly he realized what bothered him. The *Argo* didn't seem to be moving. The deck beneath his feet felt as steady as rock. He might have been standing ashore.

He knew what that meant, and he winced. The ship had run aground, and it was his fault, because he had abandoned the rudder. Then he shrugged a little; no matter what he'd done, the results would have been bad. Lose Jason or wreck the ship—he knew he'd made the right choice. A ship could be replaced; friends could not. Nothing remained but to make the best of things. Would they be stranded on some desolate island, never to be rescued? Hopefully not; Theseus might be able to fix the *Argo*, since he knew something of shipbuilding. Theseus seemed to know a little about everything. And they still had the two small boats . . .

He wouldn't worry about it now, though. First they had to make it through the storm. *At least Jason is alive,* he thought. That was the most important thing. If they lost the ship, well, they would simply have to find or build another.

A huge wave had been approaching the ship, and now it broke across the port-side railing, sending a rushing torrent of water everywhere. He spotted a length of rope tied to the starboard railing, wrapped it around his wrist and braced himself. This time, though, the water came only to his waist. Maybe there were some advantages to being grounded after all.

Turning, he gazed down at the churning sea and thought about the moment they had struck land. He hadn't heard any splintering noises . . . did that mean they had hit a beach or a sandbar? He allowed himself a moment of hope. If so, they might be able to float free later.

Since nothing could be done at the rudder, he dropped the rope and rejoined the others at the door to Jason's cabin. Orpheus and Theseus each had one of Jason's arms over their shoulder, but Jason seemed to be recovering rapidly—he had set his feet stubbornly and begun to argue with them.

"I have . . . to know . . . what happened . . ." Jason gasped.

"Easy there," Hercules said. "You're in no shape to do anything yet." Jason looked more like one of the walking dead than their heroic captain.

"But . . . the ship . . ."

"We're firmly aground," Hercules said, "and I don't think we're going anywhere soon. Now stop playing the hero and get in your cabin. You almost drowned out there!'' With that, he picked Jason up and carried him inside.

Orpheus and Theseus followed, grinning. Jason did not look happy, Hercules thought. But he didn't argue anymore.

"I'll see to him," Orpheus said. "You two find out what happened below."

"I want a full report in ten minutes!" Jason added, sounding a little stronger.

"As soon as possible," Hercules agreed.

He followed Theseus from the cabin. Outside, the storm's wrath seemed to have lessened slightly. Perhaps it was his imagination, or perhaps it was because they had run aground, but the waves no longer seemed so high and the rain no longer seemed to pound down so mercilessly.

Shielding his eyes, Hercules peered into the darkness, but he saw no lights ahead of them. Whatever Jason had seen, it wasn't here, he thought. Then another flash of lightning revealed dark trees fifty yards ahead, their branches twisting like serpents in the wind.

He caught Theseus's arm and pointed. "Land!" There would be food and water at least if they were stranded.

"I saw it, too!" Theseus said. Turning, he slid open the hatch set in the middle of the deck and climbed down into the ship's hold, where the galley and passenger quarters lay.

Hercules hurried after him, pausing only long enough to pull the hatch shut before another wave swept over the ship. No sense letting water pour into the hold.

A few small oil lamps hung by their handles from beams overhead, burning smokily and providing a wan yellow light. Everyone below—the remaining fifty-two members of the expedition—had clustered around Theseus, calling anxiously for news as to what had happened. Theseus held up his hands for silence. Everyone grew quiet.

"We ran aground," he said loudly. "We don't know

if it's a beach or a sandbar yet, just that we're stuck. Hopefully, we can ride out the storm, then float the ship free.''

Hercules asked, ''Is there any damage to the ship down here?''

Atalanta said, ''One of the oil lamps spilled, but we put out the fire.''

''Good,'' Theseus said. ''Did you check all the seams to see if we're taking on water, though? That's my main concern right now.''

Mutters came from all around. Everyone exchanged puzzled looks.

''I see,'' Hercules said. ''Nobody checked.'' He turned to Theseus. ''You look forward, I'll look aft. Shout if you find anything.''

''Right,'' Theseus said, starting toward the front of the ship.

Hercules turned and made his way between pallets to the hatch at the back of the compartment. It opened onto a short passage, with more hatches to either side. These led to storage compartments. He checked them one by one and grew increasingly optimistic—there was not a sign of damage.

Then, when he opened the last one, he saw water flooding in from somewhere behind the large clay jars, called *pithoi*, that held the ship's water supply. Six inches of water already covered the compartment floor.

''We're taking on water!'' he called.

Theseus came running, followed by the rest of the crew. Everyone peered around him at the flooding compartment. Quite a few groaned.

''It doesn't look so bad,'' Theseus said, wading in. He threw himself down in the water and wriggled behind the first *pithos*.

''What about the rest of the ship?'' Hercules asked.

''The galley and forward compartments are intact,'' Theseus called. ''Get buckets. Everyone form a line—

we're going to have to bail it out while I work.''

Hylas and Atalanta opened another compartment and began handing out goatskin buckets. A line of bailers formed. They began scooping up the water and passing it out into the main hold, then up the ladder.

"Aha!" Theseus cried. "I see the problem!"

"Well?" Hercules said. "What happened?"

"It's not as bad as it looks," Theseus reported, crawling out. "A seam split. I can force the boards back into place and seal them. But it's going to take several hours, and when I'm done, it's going to have to dry for most of a day. Then we can paint it with pitch."

Hercules sighed in relief. "Can you see to it on your own, or do you need me?"

"I can do it. You tell Jason."

"Right!"

Turning, Hercules made his way past the line of people bailing out the compartment, climbed up through the open hatch and emerged onto the deck. The storm had finally broken, and though a mistlike rain still fell, the wind had died and the waves no longer beat quite so fiercely at the *Argo*. And, he saw, the clouds to the west had already begun to break up, showing a few stars. Good news indeed.

He opened the door to Jason's cabin. "Jason?" he called softly.

Snores answered him. *Let Jason rest,* he thought as he eased the door closed. After all, their captain had almost drowned.

The line of men passing buckets up from the hold ran to the other side of the ship. He went over to join them. It looked like it was going to be a very long night.

FIVE

HERCULES WOKE THE NEXT MORN-
ing to near silence. He blinked,
and for an instant he thought
something had gone horribly wrong.

Then he remembered that the ship wasn't moving because it had grounded itself. With a groan, he pulled himself to his feet, stretched till his bones creaked, then
slowly began to make his way toward the hatch, stepping
around the dozens of sleeping men in the hold. They were
exhausted after having bailed all night.

Like them, he had spent hours passing bucket after
bucket of water while Theseus worked to fix the hull.
Finally, well after midnight, the seam had been closed.
Then, using ballast, anchor weights, and wooden braces,
Theseus had wedged the boards into position. He planned
on caulking the seams tomorrow if the weather was fair.

Hercules climbed the ladder from the hold and when
he pushed open the hatch, he blinked as a sudden burst

of sunlight hit him. The storm had ended, leaving brilliant blue skies behind. Not a single cloud marred the perfection of the heavens, though a few white-and-gray seagulls circled and swooped, giving raucous cries. The air tasted crisp and fresh.

On deck, he lowered his gaze to the island ahead of them. It had smooth, sandy beaches sprinkled with seaweed and bits of shell and driftwood that the storm had washed ashore. Beyond lay a thick, lush tangle of trees, vines, and bushes. Farther back rose a mountain; mist shrouded its jagged peak.

He noticed Jason standing in the bow, staring toward shore with a thoughtful expression on his face. He was the only one on deck now. Hercules hurried forward and joined him.

"You should get your rest," Jason told him. "Theseus told me what happened last night. You worked harder than everyone else."

Hercules shrugged modestly. "It's past dawn. I'll rest tonight. Besides, what of you? You nearly drowned."

"I feel fine now . . . thanks to you."

"You would have done the same for me." Hercules stifled a sudden yawn as he scanned the beach again. The island looked deserted, he thought. He saw no signs of people, not a house nor a hovel, not so much as a wisp of smoke from a cook fire. "Do you think it's inhabited?"

"I haven't seen anyone yet," Jason said.

"But the lights—"

"They might have come from the mountain. Or from a different island."

Hercules squinted at the mountain. Thick green forests covered its slopes halfway up; then scrub and brush took over. Here and there he spotted openings that could only be caves. Nothing moved there.

"Savages?" he asked.

"I don't know. Possibly. I have no idea of where we

are. We'll have to get our bearings from the stars tonight. Hopefully, we're not too far off course.''

''It was quite a storm.''

Jason grinned. ''If I didn't know better, I'd say one of the gods doesn't like us.''

''Doesn't like *me*, you mean.'' Hercules shook his head; he had a long-standing feud with Hera, the Queen of the Gods. But what was done could not be undone. They would have to make the best of it.

''What's your plan?'' he asked, to change the subject.

''I want to go ashore later—'' Jason began.

Movement caught Hercules' eye, and silently he pointed up the beach. It seemed they weren't alone here after all. Three children—two boys and a girl—had just come into view. The boys wore pale-blue loincloths, and the girl wore a light-green tunic. They seemed to be looking for anything that the storm had washed ashore; Hercules saw them pick up several shells and a few odd-shaped pieces of driftwood. They were so intent on searching the beach that they scarcely looked up.

''Not savages, at least,'' Jason murmured, leaning his elbows on the railing the better to watch them.

Hercules cupped his hands to his mouth. ''Ho there!'' he shouted as loudly as he could.

The three children jumped like startled rabbits, then stared. The two boys rushed forward, and after a second's hesitation, the girl followed. As they drew close, Hercules saw that the boys—one perhaps six years old, the other nine or ten—had olive skin, dark-brown eyes, and short, curly black hair. The girl, perhaps seven or eight, with her hair pulled back in a ponytail, resembled them very closely; she had to be their sister.

''Who are you?'' the older boy called. His voice held a strange, lilting accent, pleasing to the ear but like none Hercules had ever heard before. At least they spoke Greek. There was no telling how far the storm had carried the *Argo*, he realized. They could be many hundreds of miles from home.

"I am Hercules and this is Jason, the captain of this ship," Hercules called down. "We are travelers and adventurers on a great quest. What is your name, lad?"

"Morvé. This is my brother Ippe—that's short for Ippenereus—and she's Cleran, our sister."

"What island is this?" Jason called.

"Thorna," Morvé replied. Turning, he pointed back the way they had come. "Our village is over there, by the harbor. Why didn't you bring your ship there? Are you stuck?"

"For the moment," Hercules said. "We'll float it free later."

Jason asked, "What is the name of your king?"

"King?" Morvé looked puzzled. "What is that?"

Hercules said, "Your ruler. The one who guides and protects you."

"Everyone pays tribute to Gryx the Terrible. Is that who you mean?"

Hercules exchanged a glance with Jason. He had never heard of Gryx the Terrible . . . it had to be some local tyrant, he thought.

"Yes," Jason said slowly. "I would like to meet this Gryx the Terrible. Will you show us where he lives?"

Shuddering, Morvé backed away. He had a frightened look in his eyes, almost as though Jason had asked him to do something too terrifying for words. Turning, the children sprinted back the way they had come, bare feet kicking up sand.

Hercules threw back his head and laughed. "What a great man this Gryx must be," he said sarcastically, "to strike such fear in the hearts of little boys and girls!"

Jason said, "Get weapons and rouse a couple of the men. We'll take a walk to the village . . . I don't feel like waiting for Gryx the Terrible to come to us."

*   *   *

Twenty minutes later, Hercules helped Jason, Orpheus, and Atalanta lower a boat. His great muscles strained as he played out the rope, and the wooden pulleys squeaked and squealed like a pig, but soon the rowboat splashed into the water. Easy enough, he thought. Still holding the rope, he swung down to the rower's bench, then pulled the little craft close to the *Argo*. He offered his hand to the first person about to board—Atalanta.

Smiling, she hopped down unaided. She had a bow slung over her shoulder, but she carried hunting arrows rather than the longer, fiercely barbed war arrows she used in battle. Jason and Orpheus swung down after her. Each wore a short bronze sword at his side, but no shield or armor.

"Do not forget this," Theseus said from the deck, holding out a spear for Hercules.

"I won't need it," Hercules said.

"Famous last words," Atalanta said from beside him. "Don't play brave on *my* account."

"Very well, then." Shrugging, Hercules accepted the weapon and set it in the bottom of the boat. It was a hunting spear . . . they wanted to show their teeth, he knew, not march in like a conquering army. Hunting weapons should do nicely. And maybe they would have a chance to look for game on the way back.

"We should return within two hours," Jason called up to Theseus. "If it's more than four, send help."

The older man said, "There is little you could do here now, anyway. As soon as the men are rested, I will set them to unloading the ship. That will float it free. We should be loose by noon, the gods willing. Then we'll work on caulking the seams and making her seaworthy again."

Jason gave a brusque nod. "Send a runner if you have any problems."

Hercules had taken up the oars. Fitting them into the locks, he began to row strongly toward shore, and in a few minutes he heard the boat's keel scrape on sand. Shipping the oars, he leaped out waist-deep in the water and pulled the small boat safely onto the beach.

"That's one good thing about traveling with you," Atalanta told him with a grin as she hopped out onto the sand. "I don't have to get my feet wet."

"No problem, my lady." He gave her an elaborate courtly bow, and she laughed in delight.

"Sir, you surprise me."

"Let's get moving," Jason said impatiently. He started up the beach in the direction the children had gone.

"That's our Jason, all business," Atalanta muttered.

"He has accomplished more in the last year than most men do in a lifetime," Hercules replied.

"But you'd think he'd take a few minutes to relax now and then."

Hercules laughed. "True. We'll have to work on that."

Together they followed after Jason and Orpheus. Hercules had seen Jason get this way before . . . and he blamed it on the impatience of youth. Jason couldn't wait to find the Golden Fleece and finish their quest.

They walked for half an hour, passing beautiful beach after beautiful beach. The white sand gleamed; gulls and terns cawed and circled overhead. The thick, junglelike growth of trees and branches made the place seem desolate, even though Hercules knew now that people lived on the island.

Finally, rounding a spit of sand, they came upon a natural harbor where several dozen small boats lay at anchor. It was a good-sized fishing village, with perhaps five or six hundred tidy little houses built around a broad central square. Two or three thousand people must live here, Hercules estimated.

The storm seemed to have done a great deal of damage, though. Everywhere he looked, he saw people at work. Hundreds of men and women sat or stood on roofs, fixing the thatch, or clearing away branches and sundry debris.

Others worked at cleaning the streets, helping to chop up the dozens of trees that had fallen, or repairing fishing nets. They were so intent on their tasks that they hadn't even gone out fishing, Hercules saw with surprise. That struck him as odd: all the fishermen he knew went to sea every day, whether jobs needed to be done ashore or not. After all, the whole village had to eat.

"There's one of our little friends," Jason said, nodding toward the far side of the square.

Hercules spotted Morvé talking to an elderly man with a long white beard. The boy was gesturing wildly and pointing up the beach, and the old man kept nodding.

"If that's Gryx," Hercules said, "he doesn't look so terrible."

"Perhaps it's an honorary title," Jason said dryly.

"Let's introduce ourselves," Atalanta said. "No sense standing around here waiting for them to notice us."

"And I could use a drink," Hercules added. "All that walking has given me a powerful thirst."

"Very well." Taking a deep breath, Jason strode briskly and purposefully toward the square. Hercules fell into step behind him, then followed Atalanta, then Orpheus.

Quickly the villagers began to notice them. Dropping their work, they called to one another, and everyone turned to stare. In the square, a crowd soon gathered behind the old man, who put his hands on the boy's shoulders and turned him around to face Jason and the others.

"That's them!" Morvé said loudly. "Just like I said. Right, Grandfather?"

Jason bowed to the old man. "Honored sir," he said, "I am Prince Jason of Thessaly, and these are my friends and companions." Quickly he introduced Hercules, Atalanta, and Orpheus.

The old man nodded, but continued to peer suspiciously at them. "I am Uram, the elder here. On behalf of all

Thorna, I bid you welcome. Will you join me for wine and bread?"

"Of course," Jason said with a winning smile. "I am eager to learn more of your village."

"And I am eager to hear what has brought you to our land, Prince Jason. We do not see many ships here. Except for the trader Cthaeron, who comes every spring with his red-sailed ship from Syria, you are the first to visit our shores in nearly twenty years." He turned and indicated a nearby building. "This way."

"After you, sir," Jason said.

The old man nodded and led the way.

Hercules found Atalanta grinning at him as they followed. He regarded her blankly. Had he done something to amuse her?

"What is it?" he finally whispered.

"I bet they've never heard of you!" she said.

"So?"

"You'll only have charm and good looks on your side this time!"

"If that's a challenge—" he began.

"It is!"

Hercules laughed. "Then I'll gladly take you up on it."

A friendly rivalry had grown between them during their visit to Troy. Unfortunately for Atalanta, everything she did there had been attributed to Hercules by the Trojans simply because of his almost legendary reputation as a great hero. She had become more than a little frustrated at the time, he remembered. But it hadn't been *his* fault. If anything, he had tried twice as hard to give her credit for all she did.

Here, though, these people would judge them not by their reputations, but by their actions. And he planned on staying ahead of her this time. She was quite a warrior . . . he looked forward to the competition.

They trailed Jason and Uram to one of the small buildings facing the square. At the door, Hercules stepped aside with a half bow, letting Atalanta enter before him, and she gave him a smile he found enigmatic. He frowned a bit. Why did she always seem one step ahead of him?

He followed her in, then paused in the doorway, looking around in surprise. It seemed more a spice shop than a tavern. Bundles of dried herbs hung from the rafters and the walls, and he caught the rich, earthy smells of thyme, oregano, bay leaves, and other seasonings.

Several small tables sat in the center of the room. Uram crossed to one and motioned for everyone to join him. Only when each of them had found a seat did he turn to the door behind the small counter.

"Drink!" he called. "We have visitors, Lyr!"

"Coming!" a gravely voice called. A moment later a stoop-shouldered man of advancing years shuffled out. He peered at everyone from under shaggy white eyebrows. "Strangers?"

"Travelers from distant lands," Uram said.

"But the Day of Choosing—"

Hercules noticed Uram shake his head almost imperceptibly. Lyr shrugged a little, grew silent, and shuffled to the counter, where he began pulling out small red-clay bowls. He had to dust them out; clearly, they hadn't been used in some time . . . perhaps not since those Syrian traders had visited, Hercules thought. Lyr filled the bowls with deep-red wine from a clay jar under the counter, then carried them over, along with loaves of a flat dark bread.

"A toast to your island," Jason said, raising his bowl.

Everyone echoed his words, then sipped. It was a poor vintage, Hercules discovered, thin and nearly tasteless, and it had been watered down too much. But it was doubtless the best these people had to offer. He made a point of smacking his lips happily. Sure enough, Lyr beamed at him.

"Excellent," Jason said, wiping his mouth. He broke off a piece of bread and passed the rest around the table. "It is good to find a kindly welcome here," he said. "Too many people forget the common courtesies."

"We are poor," Uram said, "but we do our best. Now please, you must tell me what has brought you to our small island."

"Have you ever heard of the Golden Fleece?"

Uram frowned. "No, I don't believe so."

"Many years ago in Thessaly, my homeland," Jason said, "there lived a king named Athamas who grew to dislike his wife, so he divorced her and took another. The former queen suspected danger to her children from their new stepmother, a beautiful but cruel woman, so she prayed to the god Hermes for assistance. Hermes, moved by her plight, sent a giant ram with a golden fleece to her. She set her two children on the ram's back, trusting that the beast would carry them to safety."

Jason took another sip of wine. "Instantly the ram vaulted into the air," he continued, "carrying the two children swiftly to the East, until, when crossing the strait that divides Europe and Asia, the girl fell from its back into the sea and drowned."

"The gods can be cruel as well as kind," Uram murmured.

"Never slowing or seeming to tire," Jason went on, "the ram continued its flight until it reached the kingdom of Colchis on the eastern shore of the Black Sea, where it landed with the boy, whose name was Phryxus.

"As soon as Phryxus found himself safe, he sacrificed the ram to Zeus. Then he gave its Golden Fleece to Æetes, the king of Colchis, who placed it in a consecrated grove under the care of a sleepless dragon. For that great gift, King Æetes made Phryxus welcome in Colchis, and eventually he adopted the boy as his own son."

"An interesting tale," Uram said, leaning back and regarding Jason a little suspiciously. "But what does this Golden Fleece have to do with you?"

"I have vowed to win the Golden Fleece for my own people," Jason said. "Since the days of King Athamas,

Thessaly has been beset with bad fortune. We have suffered more than our share of famines, plagues, and crop failures. A symbol of divine power such as the Golden Fleece would surely bless our kingdom once more.''

"Possibly," Uram said, nodding.

"Beyond that," Jason said, "I need the Golden Fleece to win my own throne."

Hercules added, "Jason is Prince of Thessaly and its rightful king—though his uncle, Pelias, now rules." Pelias was a cold, hard man who had grown used to power and did not want to give it up. "Jason hopes to save his country from a civil war by returning as a hero from this great quest."

"I do have a legitimate claim to the Golden Fleece," Jason added. "My great-grandfather and Phryxus were cousins. Since King Æetes died long ago, and his direct descendants no longer rule Colchis, by rights the Golden Fleece should go to me."

"I doubt that they will feel that way," Uram said, "but I wish you luck in your endeavor."

"There is more to the story," Atalanta said.

"Oh?"

She said, "Jason sent invitations to all the adventurous young men and women of Greece, and soon he found himself joined by many famous heroes."

"Such as . . . ?"

"Hercules is probably the most famous." She nodded to him, and Hercules shrugged modestly. Enough people sang his praises without her adding to them.

"Alas, I have never heard of him . . . or of any of you. Seldom do we have news of the outside world." Uram motioned for more wine. Lyr shuffled over and began re-filling the bowls. "I wish you success in your voyage. You will leave us now?"

"Soon," Jason said.

"We thought you were Gryx the Terrible," Hercules

said suddenly. Perhaps they could find out more of this tyrant . . . and the "Day of Choosing" that the barkeeper had mentioned.

"No, he does not live here."

"Young Morvé said your village paid tribute to him."

"Oh?" Uram frowned. "The young are often confused by such things. It is not tribute—we pay for his protection."

"Who is he?" Atalanta asked, leaning forward eagerly. "Where does he live?"

Hercules added, "And what sort of tribute does he demand?"

"He is . . ." The old man hesitated as if trying to decide how to explain a very complicated matter.

Suddenly a loud crashing noise came from outside. Hercules sprang from his seat. It sounded like something large had fallen. He glanced at the others, then rushed to the door. Atalanta followed on his heels.

Outside, he found that all the villagers had dropped their tasks and now faced the mountain. They were wearing uneasy expressions. He turned, his eyes searching among the trees on the mountain's slopes, then among the crags and boulders of its heights.

Finally he spotted movement in the mouth of a cave about halfway up. Slowly, as he watched, a creature half emerged. Roughly man-shaped, it would have towered far over the tallest human who ever lived. It had to be more than twenty feet tall, he thought, and it had knotted arms like tree trunks, a huge barrel chest, and long, thick legs. Its face looked vaguely human but lumpy, as if half formed from clay. A thick black shag of beard grew around its mouth, and its hair hung down in ratty knots.

But what drew Hercules' gaze was the one huge eye set in the middle of its forehead. Slowly the creature blinked, then threw back its head and roared. The sound carried even to where they stood.

"That," Uram said heavily, "is Gryx."

"A cyclops . . ." Atalanta whispered half to herself. Hercules glanced at her. Had she ever faced a cyclops? He hadn't, but the prospect of fighting one made his heart race.

"I thought they were all dead," Jason said, and Hercules heard the awe in his voice. "Nobody has seen one in years."

Orpheus said, "There must be a few left in the corners of the world, such as Thorna. I thought they were supposed to be intelligent. This one looks little more than a beast."

"A beast he may be," Uram said, "but Gryx protects us. You must leave here now. Soon he will come for the Choosing."

Atalanta turned to him. "This 'Choosing'—what exactly *is* it?"

"Every year Gryx takes twelve of us to live with him," Morvé piped up from behind them, as if everyone knew it. "He eats one each month until they are gone, then returns for twelve more."

"That's horrible!" Hercules said. He couldn't believe the villagers put up with it. "Surely you could drive him off—"

"It is an honor to be chosen," Uram said stiffly. "This way, the village is safe."

On the mountain, the cyclops roared again. Then it ducked back inside the cave. Silence fell.

Jason shuddered in horror. "Like the minotaur in Crete," he said. "This is an abomination!"

"Surely you can kill this monster," Hercules said to Uram. "You must have two or three hundred men capable of fighting. We can help—"

Uram glared. "Kill Gryx? And have the wrath of the gods descend on us again? No—Gryx is all that protects us!"

"But your children—" Atalanta cried. "How can you lose them?"

"It is better to sacrifice a few each year to Gryx than to lose them all to the gods," Uram said firmly. He raised his head, and Hercules saw a fierce determination in his eyes. "Enough of this talk," he said firmly. "You must leave our village now, before Gryx finds you here. He would be angry. Go. Take your ship, take your people, and go!"

"So be it," Jason said curtly. He gestured for everyone to follow him and turned toward the beach and the *Argo*.

"But, Jason—" Hercules and Atalanta each called.

"I have never turned my back on danger," Hercules said. He set his feet stubbornly, hands on his spear. He wasn't about to give up so easily. Not when there was a monster to be slain.

"Uram has made his wishes clear," Jason said. "We must listen to them." He gave Hercules a long look, then jerked his head toward the *Argo*. "Back to our ship. By my father's ten thousand mules, we'll catch the next favorable wind, I swear it!"

By his father's ten thousand mules? His father didn't have any mules—

Then Hercules understood: Jason wanted to talk about it in private. A fake oath could not be binding. Hercules slowly gave a nod, as if resigning himself to their leader's decision. Of course, keeping their plans secret made more sense. They didn't want Uram warning Gryx, after all. It was always best to take a monster by surprise. He began to smile inwardly. This was the sort of adventure he liked most of all.

"We can't just walk away from these people!" Atalanta insisted. "We have a duty—"

"You have a duty to mind your own business!" Uram snapped. "Go! Go now before Gryx decides to devour *you*!"

Atalanta gave Hercules an imploring look, but in front of Uram and the village onlookers, he couldn't do more than shrug. "It is their affair," he told her, wincing inwardly. "Listen to Jason's words carefully. You swore to follow him when you set out on this quest, after all."

"So you're all going to walk away?" Atalanta demanded. "None of you will stop this cyclops?" She stared at each of them in turn. Hercules noticed that only he met her gaze. Orpheus and Jason looked down, or off to the distance, or out to sea. Atalanta gave a derisive snort. "Some band of heroes."

"It's time we got back to the *Argo*," Jason said almost meekly.

"Wait," a woman's voice called.

Hercules turned. An old woman dressed in white, carrying a small bundle wrapped in gray cloth, pushed through the crowd. The years had creased her face, but not dimmed the fire in her eyes. Around her neck she wore a necklace made of fish bones that had been carved into the shape of owls.

"Witta—" Uram said with a sigh.

"Last night," Witta proclaimed loudly, "the goddess Athena spoke to me. She bade me join these strangers on their quest. She said they would help us all."

Hercules felt his heart starting to pound with excitement. They might be able to rally the villagers against the cyclops after all.

"How is this possible?" Uram demanded.

"Do you question a goddess?" Witta asked almost scornfully.

"No. But neither do I trust one. The gods deserted Thorna long ago, Witta. Only Gryx protects us now."

Around him, others echoed those words.

Witta raised her head and looked at Jason. "Prince, my goddess has bidden me join your company. Will you take me with you?"

Jason bit his lip, and Hercules could see him weighing everything in his mind. At last he nodded.

"We have room," he told her. "You may join us."

"Thank you."

Turning again, Jason led the way back toward the beach. Witta marched behind him, Orpheus following. Atalanta brought up the rear.

Hercules slowed down until he matched Atalanta's stride, saying nothing. He couldn't believe how naïve she had been—hadn't she picked up on Jason's intentions? The oath by his father's ten thousand mules had been a clear giveaway.

As soon as they were out of Uram's sight, Atalanta gave Hercules a wink. "What did you think of my performance?" she asked slyly.

Hercules stopped. "Performance?"

"In the village. Jason gave up too easily, and I thought it might make Uram suspicious. I was just trying to make our departure more convincing."

Hercules sighed in relief. "Good!" he said. "You had me worried. I thought you were about to charge off and fight that monster single-handedly."

She laughed. "No chance of that this time. I'm not crazy." She frowned. "Have you ever fought a cyclops?"

"No. But it can't be that hard. They *are* mortal, after all." He thought back to what he knew about them. They were creatures from the first days of the Earth, when the Titans had ruled. They had been banished to the far corners of the world when Zeus overthrew his parents and seized rulership of the Earth.

Rounding the spit of land separating the village from the beach where the *Argo* had run aground, Hercules shaded his eyes, peering ahead at the ship. He could see movement on the *Argo*: boats being loaded, then rowed to shore. Theseus must be trying to get as much weight off as possible to help her float free.

Suddenly the *Argo* began to move, rolling slightly with the waves, and the sailors ran up one small sail. Slowly, like a wounded seal, the proud ship glided twenty feet out, into deeper waters. There, as everyone on board cheered, anchors splashed into the low waves to hold the ship in place.

Jason paused, and they gathered around. Hercules regarded Witta a trifle suspiciously. What would happen when she found out they meant to kill Gryx and free her people? Would she run back and try to warn everyone?

"It seems our ship is free," Jason said, looking at the old woman. Hercules knew then that Jason shared his suspicions. "We can sail on now . . . as soon as we take care of a few tasks, like finding fresh water."

"There is a small spring just inland." Witta pointed slightly to the left. "But first you must kill Gryx. Uram is a fool. The monster must be destroyed, and as quickly as possible."

Hercules grinned. "You are a wise woman indeed," he said. She inclined her head slightly in his direction.

"Do you know how Gryx may be slain?" Jason asked her.

"I have seen him bleed," she said. "When he first swam to Thorna some thirty years ago, we fought him off for many months. He stole sheep and goats to survive. I know he can be killed, if you have the courage and the strength."

"We do!" Hercules vowed.

"Then arm yourselves. Soon he will come to the village and make his choosing. After he returns to his cave, he will fall into a deep sleep. Then you must strike." She smiled, her eyes distant. "Long have I dreamed of this day! Freedom is at hand!"

"Very well," Jason said. "I'll take ten men."

"And me," Atalanta said sharply.

Jason nodded. "Of course," he said apologetically. "Nine men and you, Atalanta. Now let's get back to the ship. Theseus may need our help . . . and we have to find a cabin for Witta."

"Look!" Atalanta pointed to the mountain.

Hercules whirled. Trees had begun to topple below the cave of the cyclops . . . the monster was making its way toward the village.

SIX

"GRYX IS COMING," URAM INTONED, watching the mountain. At his side, Morvé stared up at the thick trees, too. Suddenly one fell with a crash, then another, then another: the cyclops was shoving them out of its path as it made its way down toward the village.

Morvé swallowed. This would be his first year to take part in the Choosing. He felt a sick dread running through his body and tried not to let it show. Uram was his grandfather as well as the village elder. Morvé knew that he had to set an example for all the other eligible people in Thorna.

A horn began to sound, its low, mournful note carrying throughout the village. It summoned everyone to the Choosing. Morvé knew that all the people would be laying down their tasks, gathering up their children, and heading to the center of the square.

Uram knelt before him and gave him a hug. "My sweet

boy," he said, and Morvé saw tears in his eyes. "May Gryx spare you," he whispered.

"Do not worry about me," Morvé said. "If it is the gods' will, I will be spared."

He glanced toward the mountain. Now he could hear the cyclops' approach: the thunderous crash of trees being knocked aside, the shrill cries of birds, the screams and angry chatter of squirrels.

"To your places!" Uram cried, and Morvé watched him rise and move to the center of the square. "Assemble! Everyone to your places!"

Men and women scrambled across the village square. All the ones who might be chosen—the boys and girls between the ages of twelve and sixteen—gathered around Morvé. He saw that several of them had been crying. He swallowed and found a lump in his own throat.

Uram is depending on me, he told himself. *I have to show the others how brave I am. I have to stand tall and proud, even if Gryx chooses me.*

"Line up!" he told the others firmly. Giving him sullen looks, they obeyed: boys to one side, girls to the other. He counted nineteen boys and twenty-two girls. Six of each would be chosen. Since Gryx usually took the tallest and fattest, Morvé did not think he would be chosen this year. But everyone said he was tall for his age, so next year, or the year after, he might well be one of those selected.

With a roar, Gryx appeared outside the village. Morvé swallowed again, this time in sudden terror. The cyclops stood nearly twenty-five feet tall, towering over the houses and shops. When it saw the crowd in the center of the square, it gave a nasty bark of laughter.

I will not be chosen this year, Morvé whispered to himself. *I will not be afraid.*

Slowly Gryx made his way forward.

"Hungry!" he bellowed.

Uram hurried forward, throwing himself on the ground before the cyclops.

"Great Gryx!" he cried. "We thank you for another year of protection! In reward, we offer you our blood—the pick of our children!"

"Hungry *now*!" Gryx bellowed. "Take *now*!"

The cyclops strode forward. The ground shook with its every step. Morvé's head did not even come to the creature's knee. He gazed up, up, up, past the thickly matted tangle of hair on its legs, past its crude kilt, past its thick barrel chest. The monster's mouth gaped; ropes of saliva glistened amid rotted black teeth. Its breath stank of carrion.

"You—you—you—" The creature's hand pointed at the three tallest boys, who stood in the back with their heads down. They had known they would be chosen this year. They had already said good-bye to their parents. "You—you—" The cyclops' eye lingered for a second on Morvé. "You!"

Morvé felt his heart pause as the cyclops pointed at him. He had been chosen. He would have to accompany Gryx back to the mountain, to be eaten. A shrill ringing filled his ears. *I must be brave,* he told himself. *I must show the others how strong we can be.*

Suddenly his legs went weak and he nearly fell. The boys next to him, who had been spared, seized his arms and propped him up. They were almost crying. Around the square, men and women *were* crying. Morvé managed to turn his head. His mother had thrown herself to the ground. Slowly she pounded the dirt with her fists, shrieking in anguish. His father looked sick. Then Morvé saw his grandfather standing in the center of the square, tears running down his cheeks, a stunned look on his face.

Morvé turned his back on them. *I have to be strong,* he told himself again. Squeals of fear came from the line of girls as Gryx moved to examine them. "You—you—

you," the cyclops grunted, pointing until it had selected six.

Morvé barely heard the new screams and cries of lamentation from the parents of those who had been selected. Numbly, hardly able to think, he joined the group of twelve gathering behind the cyclops.

Grinning, Gryx turned and—slowly now, so they could keep up—began the long march back to his cave at the top of the mountain. Morvé stumbled and fell repeatedly, but he barely felt the raw cuts on his knees and hands.

He had been chosen. He must be strong.

SEVEN

G ATHER AROUND!'' JASON CRIED TO the workers on the beach as he sprinted up to them.

Hercules, Orpheus, and Atalanta followed right on his heels. When Hercules glanced back, he found Witta hurrying as fast as she could.

Quickly the crew formed a semicircle around Jason. There were anxious expressions on all. Everyone else had spotted the cyclops, too, though of course they could not yet know what Jason planned.

"There is a monster living in a cave on the mountain," Jason cried. "It is a cyclops named Gryx, who terrorizes the inhabitants of the island. Each year Gryx chooses six sons and six daughters as tribute. He takes them back to his cave and devours them."

Everyone shuddered at that. Hercules turned to watch the monster's progress. It would be in the village in a few minutes. They needed to act quickly.

"Who will help us kill it?" Hercules cried.

Everyone shouted at once that they would go. Theseus—Meleagar—every able-bodied man called out to be included. Hercules smiled grimly; yes, Jason had chosen this crew well. Even the two youths who had joined them the week before, Nalos and Hylas, cried out to come along. All wanted a share of the glory.

"We can take seven more with us," Jason said solemnly. "Theseus, I want you here, working on the *Argo*. Everyone else can draw lots to go."

Disappointed mutters came from those present, but Hercules knew it was the right decision. With too many people, they would trip over each other as they fought. As it was, eleven might prove too many. He would have chosen no more than six or seven himself. After all, five of them had slain a sea-monster twice the cyclops' size in Troy only a week before.

"To be fair to all," Hercules said, "I will prepare the lots." He crossed to a patch of scruffy, sun-yellowed grass atop a nearby dune and pulled out two handfuls of long, coarse stalks. They were as thick and hard as straw. He carefully broke seven of them in half, mixed them in with the rest, and returned to the group.

"Draw," he said, holding them out. His large hand hid the small ones among the larger straws. "The seven shortest will go."

After a second's hesitation, Orestes stepped forward and drew first, then cursed and threw his to the sand.

"Not my lucky day," he said with a disappointed sigh. "I'll miss all the fun."

"There's still plenty to do here," Theseus reminded him. "We have those seams to caulk, remember."

"Oh, that's *very* exciting," Orestes muttered under his breath. Hercules tried to hide his grin and failed. Everyone else was laughing, too. Shaking his head, Orestes joined Theseus to one side.

"Who will be next?" Hercules called. He offered the handful of grass to Telamon.

"No, no," the warrior said with a laugh. "It's bad luck to draw early. I'll go last."

"We'll go next," a small voice said, almost timidly.

Hercules turned. Hylas had spoken. He and his brother Nalos stepped forward nervously. Both were fifteen years old, with curly black hair and the down of youth still upon their cheeks, but despite their age, they had twice proved themselves in battle, helping drive off a band of bandits led by a cunning centaur named Koremos. Hercules frowned a bit at the thought. Truth to tell, the pair had belonged to Koremos's band, but they had done everything they could to put that life behind them. Both Theseus and Jason seemed to have taken a special interest in seeing them grow to become honest, noble warriors, and even Hercules had to admit the lads seemed to have set their feet upon the right path. In a few years, they might well rival Orestes, Orpheus, or any of the others here in their adventures.

Both of them drew straws. Suddenly Nalos gave a whoop and held his up for all to see. It was short. Grinning, he ran to stand beside Jason, while his brother Hylas joined Theseus and Orestes. Hylas looked heartbroken. Well, he would get over it soon enough, Hercules thought. Boys were like that.

So it went. Meleagar and Iacoros joined Jason, then Maenar and Philoran. Finally, Telamon drew the last short straw.

"I knew it!" Telamon cried. "The luck is in the last man!"

Those who had missed out muttered enviously among themselves. Still, nobody could be depressed for long, not in this company, and soon they had clustered around Jason and Hercules, patting everyone on the back and wishing them a speedy victory. Hercules laughed and promised them success.

"You will have to fight the monster in its cave," Witta said.

"What?" Hercules turned and stared inland. He saw that Gryx had begun his trek back to his cave. The cyclops' head bobbed among the treetops halfway up the mountain. That meant it must have finished choosing its victims.

Atalanta cursed. "I knew we should have made our stand in the village!" she said.

Jason turned to the priestess. "Witta," he said, "what do you know about that cave?"

"Little," she admitted. "Just that he takes his prisoners there and keeps them in a pen. He will eat one immediately, then save the rest for the coming months."

Hercules gave a startled yelp. *"Immediately?"*

She nodded. "Yes. That is his way. Then he will fall into a deep slumber . . . if you hurry, you may reach him before he wakes."

"Theseus—Orestes—" Jason called. "Get to the *Argo*. Get our weapons. Fast!"

Hercules glanced over at Jason, who had a pained look on his face. *He doesn't think we can make it fast enough,* Hercules realized. Their good weapons were still on the ship. It would take time to get them. And they still had to make it up the mountain to the cave.

He drew a deep breath. "We will have to run," he said.

Everyone staying behind hastened for the boats and began to row out to the *Argo* with frantic speed. Would it be fast enough? Somehow, Hercules didn't think so.

EIGHT

ORVÉ CLIMBED THE WINDING mountain trail first. He was determined to set an example for the others, and though it took every ounce of his strength, he managed to keep a straight face. Everyone else had begun to cry.

"Walk! Walk fast!" Gryx bellowed from behind them.

Morvé glanced back. His cousin Hallon had been chosen as well. Hallon, blubbering like an old woman, had slipped on the rocks and now lay there in a heap.

"Walk!" Gryx roared.

Morvé hesitated. None of the others moved to help, so he picked his way back to where his cousin lay.

"You have to get up," he said urgently.

"No-o-o-o!" Hallon wailed.

Morvé seized his arm and pulled him to his feet. "You don't want to make Gryx angry, do you?" he muttered. "You don't want him to eat you *here*, do you?"

Hallon shook his head.

"Then come on! Move!"

Feeling his way carefully, Hallon began to struggle up the ragged trail again. Gryx gave a grunt that might have been approval. Slowly, the line began to move.

At last they reached the cave. It was a huge thirty-foot-tall slash in the rock. A foul reek came from it—something like the stench of the butcher's shed, something like the stench of a privy, all mingled with other, even nastier odors like none Morvé had ever smelled before. He gagged and felt sick. Everyone drew up behind him, making plaintive cries.

"In!" Gryx roared.

They hesitated, looking at one another. Morvé swallowed. He didn't want to go inside either.

"*In!*" Gryx shouted again, stamping the ground like a child. The rocks trembled underfoot. Morvé had to steady himself against the stone wall of the cave to keep from falling.

He took a last gulp of clean air. He was the grandson of the village elder, he told himself. He had to lead by example, just as Grandfather Uram did. Holding his breath, he went inside. Behind him, he heard the others following.

It was dark within, and his eyes began to water. Finally he had to breathe, and he discovered that the reek was far worse in the cave. He gagged and almost threw up.

Then, as his eyes became used to the dimness, he recognized bloody clothing and human bones lying in heaps all over the floor—some with bits of rotting flesh still attached. They had to be what remained of those Gryx had taken over the years.

"There!" Gryx said, following them in. The cyclops pointed toward the back of the cave. "Now!"

Feeling numb, hardly able to think, Morvé moved forward as though in a daze. *He's going to eat us. He's going to eat us all.* At the far end of the cave sat a huge pen built from the trunks of trees. The foulest smell came from it; human waste made a nasty smear on the floor. It seemed they were to be locked up until they were eaten.

Morvé forced himself forward. His legs felt like wooden blocks. His heart pounded. Moaning, wailing, the others trailed him. All of the girls had begun to weep, and at the sound, Gryx began to chuckle deep in his throat.

When they were all inside, Gryx peered over the top of the pen. Then, in a sudden movement, he snatched up the boy next to Morvé—it was Hallon, Morvé saw—and bit his head off with one bite. The cyclops began to chew, making horrible smacking noises. Turning, still chewing, he went off to another part of the cave.

Morvé felt his knees give way. He sat in the muck and the filth, hardly able to breathe. *Why did Gryx choose me? Everyone said I was too little this year.*

It wasn't fair. But he couldn't do anything about it. He felt a tear trace a line down his cheek, then spill over the curve of his jaw.

Uram's knees felt like water. As though through a tunnel, he had watched Gryx lead this year's chosen children off toward the mountain. And his grandson went first, head high, back straight, the best and proudest of them all.

Uram wanted to scream, to cry, to rend his clothing and tear his flesh. But how could he? All these years he had told the villagers not to interfere, to let Gryx take his choices so they could all live in peace. It *had* to be this way.

After Gryx had vanished up the mountain, Uram turned and took a deep breath. Most of the villagers had gone, silently retreating to their homes. Only his own son, Ranos—a tall, dark-haired fisherman of thirty-two years—remained behind. Ranos stared at him, blue eyes hard.

"You should have listened to the strangers," Ranos said. Then he turned and stomped off toward his house.

He had a wife to comfort—and they both had a son to bury, if not in actuality yet, then at least in spirit.

Uram went to his own house, closed and bolted the door, then sagged onto a stool beside the table. Wine sat there, waiting. He had known he would need it. Now, alone, he began to drink. He wouldn't stop until his grandson's happy, laughing face left his mind.

Half an hour after Jason had chosen his men for the attack on Gryx, Hercules felt like crying in despair.

They found the trail from the beach almost impassable. Fallen trees, tangled vines, and heavy jungle growth blocked them at every turn. They hacked at the dense undergrowth with their swords, fighting for each foot they gained.

Then Hercules came to a fallen tree as thick around as his shoulders were broad. Normally he would have scrambled over it, or lifted it high enough for the others to pass safely underneath, but this time his frustration got the best of him. Setting his feet, he wrapped his powerful arms around the trunk and heaved with all his strength. Slowly it began to move, making a great creaking noise. Its roots, still partly buried, tore free as he raised it over his head. Then, in one quick movement, he hurled it to one side. The huge trunk fell with a crash, but he cared little about the sound. All he could think of were the children in the cave ahead . . . at least one of whom might be dead already, if Witta were right.

They never should have listened to the villagers, he told himself bitterly. When you saw a great evil like this cyclops, you had to strike at once. Now some boy or girl might well be dead because of their delay.

Another tree blocked their path ten feet ahead. He ran to it, seized it around the thickest part—it had to be at least a hundred years old, with a trunk even wider than the last one—and in one swift move, he heaved it to the left. It flew twenty paces before bouncing and rolling to a stop.

"Hercules—"

Panting, he paused and found Atalanta beside him. She had a concerned look on her face.

"What is it?" he demanded.

"Slow down. You won't do us any good if you're too exhausted to fight when we get there."

Hercules bit back a protest. She was right, as usual. Taking a moment to wipe the sweat from his forehead, he stopped to catch his breath. Everyone around him did the same. Half an hour of fighting through the underbrush had gotten to them, too, he saw. They had been having trouble keeping up with the pace he set.

"Five minutes," Jason said, leaning heavily on his spear. Sweat beaded on his forehead. "We're almost there."

Almost wouldn't be good enough if it cost the life of a child, Hercules thought, but he said nothing—there was no sense rushing unprepared into battle. He had lived through enough wars to know how poorly exhausted men fought. And against a cyclops, you had better fight *very* well.

"The rest of the trail looks good from here," Atalanta said, peering ahead. "We're almost to the tree line."

"Good." Hercules nodded. Another ten minutes and they could be at the cave. Hopefully, it wouldn't be too late. The seconds seemed to pass all too slowly.

Finally, Jason rose. "Quick march, double file," he called.

Atalanta had been carrying Hercules' spear for him while he cleared the trail, and he reclaimed it from her now. She took her place just behind him at the head of the column, next to Orpheus. Jason stood next to Hercules.

They began to jog, a mile-eating run. Hercules ducked under a last few branches, then they burst out into the open. The cave lay a hundred yards ahead . . . up past a few knobby outcroppings of rock.

Jason raised one hand. Everyone slowed, then stopped. Hercules found himself holding his breath and forced himself to inhale. No sounds came from ahead . . . Gryx might well be sleeping, as Witta had predicted. Or he could have spotted them from his cave. If so, he would likely be waiting in ambush.

"Atalanta," Jason whispered, "take point. Watch out for Gryx. He may be planning to surprise us."

Hercules shifted uneasily. That was a job he would have welcomed for himself, but he had to admit that Atlanta made a more logical choice. She could move as softly as a cat when she chose.

"Right." Giving Hercules a quick grin, she nocked an arrow to her bow and padded forward, silent as a ghost.

Hercules tightened his grip on his spear.

Then a slight noise from above caught his attention. He leaned back, looking up the mountain . . . to where a rock fifty yards above the cave had begun to teeter. With a jolt, he realized that Atalanta would soon be in its path.

"Look out!" he screamed. "Above you!"

Atalanta leaped back, pressing herself against the side of the mountain under a slight overhang as the huge rock fell. It gathered speed and more rocks joined it, forming a small avalanche. Dust roiled up, hiding Atalanta as the rocks poured down around her.

The cyclops peered down at them from a ledge far above. *"Kill you!"* it screamed. Its voice sounded like thunder.

Several men threw their spears, but the weapons fell short, clattering harmlessly on the rocky slopes of the mountain. Hercules knew he could throw his spear far enough to reach Gryx, but he held back. It would be too easy to miss out here. If the cyclops moved the wrong way, he would have thrown his weapon away.

"To the cave!" Jason cried. "Free the children!"

He dashed forward, and everyone followed. Hercules brought up the rear, ready to defend the others if Gryx attacked from above.

The cyclops began to roll more stones down at them, but they missed badly and thudded well behind them.

The dust had begun to settle where the avalanche had hit; Atalanta still stood under the overhang, covered in gray dust from head to foot, a dazed look on her face. Blood matted the side of her head; she must have been hit by a small stone, Hercules realized. Her glassy eyes stared through him.

"Come on!" he cried, and when she didn't even blink, he scooped her up and threw her over his shoulder, then ran as fast as he could after the others.

Jason had reached the cave's mouth. A foetid stink poured out. Hercules gagged as he set Atalanta back on her feet. By the gods, what was that reek? It was almost as bad as the Augean Stables had been. Everyone covered their mouth and nose, choking and gasping.

"A foul monster!" Jason growled. Taking a last deep breath of fresh air, he threw himself inside, rolling across the floor and then scrambling toward the far wall.

Hercules thrust Atalanta at Nalos. "Take care of her," he said. "Follow when she's able to keep up."

"Yes, sir!" the boy said.

Hercules followed Jason into the cave, and the others trailed him. Tunnels and chimneys led off in all directions; Gryx could be in any one of them, he thought.

The stench grew worse. Bones—some human, some animal—littered the ground. Excrement smeared the walls. It was like the lair of some unclean beast. Clearly, Gryx had lived for years in his own filth, piling layers of debris up around himself until they were like some disgusting nest.

"Spread out," Jason said to the others. "Watch for Gryx. Hercules and I will find the children."

A tangle of logs stood against the back wall. Suddenly

Hercules realized it was a pen . . . a huge, crude structure that the cyclops had built to hold its captives.

"They must be in there!" he said, jogging forward.

Jason joined him. It *was* a pen, Hercules realized, peering between two of the logs. He could see dark shapes moving about on the other side.

Using his spear, Jason worked at the vines binding the logs together. Hercules searched for a handhold. If he could get a strong enough grip, he might be able to pull the logs apart.

One of the children peered out at them. Hercules thought it was Morvé.

"You must leave," the boy said firmly. "We have to stay here. Gryx protects Thorna."

"He is an abomination," Hercules said. "Do you want to die?"

"No, but—"

"Then shut up!" He found a gap wide enough to get both his hands inside, then turned to Jason. "I can do it."

Jason nodded and moved back a safe distance.

Hercules shoved his hands between two logs and began to pull. He heard dry wood creak. Then one log split. Wrenching it out of the way, he pulled on the tough, thick old vines he had exposed. Unfortunately for Gryx, they had rotted in the dampness, and now they snapped like strings.

Suddenly the whole front section of the pen began to teeter. Morvé gaped through the hole in the logs.

"Move back!" Hercules shouted to the children inside. He hadn't come this far to crush them to death.

They scampered to the cave's rear wall, Morvé included. Several of the girls began crying. Fools—didn't they want to be rescued?

He gave a final push, and the pen collapsed with a crash. Across the fallen logs, he could see the children huddled together. How many were there? He squinted in the dimness, counting—*one, two, three*—

Something thudded heavily behind him. Hercules felt the hairs on the back of his neck start to prickle with alarm.

"He's coming!" Philoran shouted.

—six, seven, eight—

"He's almost here," Jason said urgently. Hercules heard the hiss of a bronze blade leaving its scabbard.

—nine, ten, eleven—

With a howl of pain, Hercules turned. *Only eleven.* One child was gone—dead, he knew. Devoured by the monster. They had come too late.

He followed Jason's gaze to the side of the cave. There, Gryx's legs could be seen. The cyclops had begun to climb down a natural chimney leading to another cave. That was probably how it had gotten above them without being seen, Hercules realized.

Philoran and Orpheus jabbed at Gryx's feet with their spears. The cyclops began to howl in pain and rage.

Hercules drew back his spear and began to take careful aim. He couldn't see the cyclops' head, but he knew that a deep wound to the stomach or back might well kill the monster.

"No!" a tiny voice shouted from behind him just as he began to throw. Then something shoved him from behind, staggering him and knocking his throw off target.

Growling in anger, he whirled. Didn't the boy know he was being rescued?

"Are you insane?" he demanded. They didn't have time for this nonsense.

"Leave Gryx alone!" Morvé launched himself at Hercules again, small fists pounding. Hercules caught the boy's hands and dragged him to the mouth of the cave.

Outside, he found Nalos peering in and shifting anxiously from foot to foot. Hercules threw Morvé to him.

"Keep him out here!" he said.

Face twisted in fury, Morvé leaped to his feet and would have thrown himself at Hercules again had Nalos not grabbed his filthy tunic and hauled him back.

"What do you want me to do?" Nalos asked.

"Sit on him!"

Nalos grinned. In one quick move, he knocked Morvé's feet out from under him and pinned him to the ground. The boy began to cry and thrash, but Nalos held him tight.

Hercules glanced at Atalanta. She sat with her head in her hands. Blood seeped between her fingers. Her eyes as she peered up at him seemed oddly large and out of focus.

"How are you?" he asked.

"My head hurts, and I can't see straight," she said. "What did you hit me with?"

"Me?" he protested. "Gryx dropped rocks on you!"

"Figures you'd find a way to hog all the monsters," she muttered. He heard a note of wry amusement in her voice, though, and knew she was joking.

"You can have the next one," he promised. That reminded him—Jason and the others were still inside.

He ran back into the cave, eyes adjusting quickly to the dimness. The rest of the children still huddled against the back wall. Good. He wouldn't have to worry about fighting them off.

Jason and the other men were clustered around the chimney. Gryx had managed to climb down to the cave floor. Whirling a club savagely, he kept them at bay. Jason, Telamon, and Orpheus jabbed with spears; Meleagar, Iacaros, and Maenar—who had thrown their spears outside—hung back with swords ready, prepared to leap in whenever a chance presented itself. The strategy seemed to be working, Hercules thought: Gryx bled from numerous wounds to his hands, stomach, and legs.

Hercules looked for the spear he'd thrown before, but it lay near Gryx's feet. That left only the logs as possible weapons . . . and they were still tied together.

Maenar leaped forward suddenly, thrusting with his sword, trying to hamstring Gryx's leg. The cyclops gave a backhanded swing that caught him in the side, and with a terrible crunch of breaking bones, Maenar flew against the wall. He sagged to the floor, dead or unconscious.

"Stop!" Hercules roared. Enough people had died. "Stop! Gryx! Jason! *Stop!*"

Gryx hesitated. Jason, Telamon, and Orpheus paused, panting. Everyone stared at him.

Hercules walked forward, arms out to show he was unarmed. The cyclops stared at him, then half raised its club.

"Smash!" the cyclops bellowed.

"Stop!" Hercules said. "Enough fighting!"

"Why?" Gryx demanded.

"I challenge you," Hercules said. "Fight *me*, Gryx, if you dare!"

"You fight me?" Gryx said. "I smash!"

"If you win, you can eat me," Hercules said firmly.

"Hercules—what are you saying?" Jason demanded in a low voice.

"I want a fair fight!" Hercules said. He faced Gryx again. "Come on, monster. Wrestle me. If you win, you can eat me. What do you say?"

"Yes!" Gryx bellowed. "I smash you!" He raised his club and started forward.

"No weapons," Hercules said firmly. "Just hands. *Wrestling*, Gryx. Not smashing. *Wrestling.*"

For a second, Gryx hesitated, then slowly he grinned as he realized what Hercules wanted. Hercules saw his jagged, rotting teeth. Grinning even wider, the monster lowered the club.

"Are you insane?" Jason demanded. "It's a *cyclops*!"

"Let me do it my way," Hercules insisted. "See to Maenar."

Then, growling low in his throat like a dog, Gryx rushed him. Hercules leaped forward.

NINE

HERCULES FEINTED TO THE RIGHT, then darted between Gryx's legs. The cyclops towered over him, and Hercules meant to use that to his advantage. He could move faster than the cyclops, and he knew it.

Off balance, Gryx tried to turn too fast and teetered for an instant. *Now—this is my chance,* Hercules thought. He spun to the side, stomped on Gryx's right foot, then threw his full weight against the monster's left leg.

Arms flailing, Gryx fell against the wall, almost crushing Telamon, who scrambled to get out of the way.

Hercules leaped onto Gryx's chest and seized the monster's throat in both hands, tightening his powerful fingers. This was how he had killed the Nemean Lion; no weapon could pierce its skin, so he'd strangled it. And this was how he had killed the pythons Hera had sent to slay him in his crib when he was an infant.

Choking, Gryx rolled to the side. Hercules let his feet

drop to the floor and he found himself propping up the cyclops, two thousand pounds of weight pressing down on him. Gritting his teeth, he tightened his grip.

Suddenly the monster opened its mouth and tried to swallow Hercules' head. Hercules ducked to one side, and the cyclops bit his shoulder.

Screaming in pain as those huge teeth tried to grind through his rocklike muscle and bone, Hercules released his stranglehold and instead thrust both arms into Gryx's mouth, forcing those huge, powerful jaws apart. Inch by inch, he pried the teeth away from him and then, in one swift movement, he ripped down and out as hard as he could. Gryx's jaw made a popping sound like a branch breaking.

Howling, the cyclops dropped and scrambled backward on hands and knees. Its jaw hung slack—dislocated, Hercules thought. Gryx would never bite anything again. Turning, the monster fled deeper into the cave.

Hercules pursued it, a hunter running a wounded stag to ground. The light grew dim as he passed into a narrow, dark chamber. Glistening stalactites hung from the ceiling, slowly dripping water. Bats rustled from high-up perches. Somewhere in the dark, Gryx began to whimper. It was one of the most pathetic sounds Hercules had ever heard, and it raised goose bumps on his arms.

"Come out," he said softly. Killing this monster would be a kindness now. "Come out, Gryx. You know you have to."

With a wet, sobbing sound, the cyclops rushed at him. No, Hercules realized an instant later, Gryx wasn't rushing *at* him, but *around* him, trying to escape.

Leaping forward, Hercules caught the monster's leg, tripping him. Gryx sprawled forward, hitting the floor with bone-jarring force. He gave a plaintive mew. The fight was over, Hercules knew. Gryx wasn't trying to kill him anymore. Flight was the only thing in his simple mind.

As Gryx tried to scramble away, Hercules leaped onto

his back, grabbed his head with both hands, and wrenched it to the side. The cyclops's neck made a sharp cracking noise as it broke. Gryx shuddered once, then slumped and didn't move.

Panting, Hercules climbed to the ground. Jason and the others hurried over and began pounding him on the back, congratulating him.

Hercules gave a grim nod. It had not been a good fight, but it had been necessary. They had lost one child . . . and probably one man. It had been too high a price.

"What of Maenar?" he asked.

Jason shook his head. "Dead," he said sadly.

"Then let's go." Hercules took a deep breath. "I want to wash this stink off. And we have to send the children home. After that, we can bury our comrade."

"Let me up," Morvé said. He had stopped struggling. By the cheers from within the cave, he knew Gryx had died. He felt a numb sort of pain inside, like the first time he'd lost a baby tooth. These strangers had saved his life. But that didn't matter now; they might just as well have killed him and saved the myserae the trouble.

"Are you going to stop fighting?" the man holding him down demanded.

"Yes. Word of honor." Morvé nodded solemnly. There wasn't any reason to fight now that Gryx had been murdered.

"All right. But watch yourself!" The man rolled off, then offered Morvé a hand up.

Morvé ignored it and climbed to his feet on his own. The others were coming out of Gryx's cave now, carrying a limp body between them. He stared, then relaxed. It was a man he had never seen before. The rest of the Chosen followed the Argonauts, looking around fearfully as if someone might come along and whisk them back into the cave to feed another cyclops. But it was too late for that now, Morvé thought. There were no other cyclops to protect them.

Turning, he gazed up at the sky. What about the myserae? Would they return now, like Grandfather Uram always said they would? Or would Thorna be spared? He allowed himself a brief moment of hope. Maybe the myserae were gone. Maybe his people didn't need Gryx's protection anymore. Maybe—

"Are you all right?" Hercules asked, bending on one knee to look him in the eyes.

Slowly, Morvé met his gaze. "Gryx ate Hallon," he said simply, "not me."

"I'm sorry. Was he a friend of yours?"

"My cousin."

"If only we had gotten here faster—"

"It doesn't matter now. We're all going to die."

Hercules looked puzzled. "Why do you say that?"

"Gryx protected us."

"From what?"

"From the myserae, of course." Hercules continued to look puzzled, so Morvé went on. "The myserae—the flesh-eaters. Grandfather Uram says they keep away from Thorna only because of Gryx."

Hercules laughed. "I haven't seen any of these flesh-eaters. I'm sure they're just stories to frighten children."

"You'll see," Morvé said solemnly. "They *are* real, and they'll be back. Especially now that Gryx is gone. They'll be back, and this time they *will* kill us all."

"First things first." Hercules stood. "Let's get you home."

Silently, Morvé turned and began to pick his way down the trail toward his village. *At least my parents will be happy—until the myserae kill us all.*

From behind, he heard the other boys and girls, and then the Argonauts, start to follow him home.

* * *

When Iacoros and Telamon carried Maenar's body out of the cave and started down the mountain on the easy path to the village, Atalanta stood too fast and had to lean against the side of the mountain to keep from falling. Shaking her head didn't help; everything swam drunkenly around her, and a ringing sound filled her ears. She staggered back and would have fallen if Hercules hadn't grabbed her arm.

"I'm fine," she protested.

"You're not fine," he told her. "Theseus should have a look at your head when we get back to the *Argo*."

"It stopped bleeding."

"That's not the point."

She sighed, pressing her eyes shut for an instant, then nodded. No sense being brave—she *was* hurt. That rock might well have cracked her skull. It couldn't hurt to have the wound properly dressed.

"I'll see him as soon as we get back," she promised. "Give me a hand down? I don't want to fall."

"Of course," he said soothingly, steadying her elbow. They started after the others.

"And don't forget your promise," she said.

"My promise?" He glanced at her, looking puzzled.

"The next monster's mine!"

He threw back his head and laughed. "You'll never change," he said. "Not even falling rocks can knock sense into you!"

She grinned feebly at him. By the gods, it hurt to be a cripple like this. Her balance had better come back, and soon, if she was going to keep up with Hercules.

Uram gazed through bleary, drunken eyes at the small figure that had appeared at the back door of his house. A ghost? It had to be. He gave a shudder, then made a quick gesture to ward off evil.

He had been drinking since Gryx's Choosing. It hadn't been enough yet. He still remembered Morvé's face.

"Grandfather—" the ghost said.

Uram staggered to his feet. The clay cup he'd been cradling fell to the floor and shattered, spilling red wine everywhere.

"I'm sorry, boy—" he said. Turning, he stumbled toward the door into his bedroom. The ghost followed, but he only turned his head away, refusing to look. "I'm sorry—it had to be. I'm sorry—" he mumbled.

"No, Grandfather, it's *me*. It's really *me*."

He raised his head slowly. "Morvé?"

"Yes, Grandfather." Morvé rushed forward and gave him a hug.

"What—how—"

"Jason and Hercules . . . they . . . they killed Gryx!"

Uram felt his legs go weak. *They promised not to.* He sat down on his bed. A sudden hole filled his chest. He couldn't breathe. *They promised to go and leave us in peace.*

"Why . . ." he whispered. "Why would they do that?"

Morvé went on. "They say there aren't any myserae. They say those are just stories to scare children."

"The myserae took my wife . . . your grandmother. They killed more than Gryx ever did. They are *real*." He shook Morvé. "Do you understand? They're *real*, and they're going to come back for us!"

"You're hurting me!"

Uram released his grandson suddenly. His head throbbed. He rubbed his eyes, trying to think.

Without Gryx, the myserae would return. He knew it. Without Gryx, they would be helpless. *But the Choosing is over. Morvé has been spared.* He bit his lip, not knowing whether to cry with joy or pain.

Finally he knelt and hugged his grandson tightly. "Go on, boy," he whispered. "Go see your mother and father. Hurry." *At least some good may come of this. Maybe my son can forgive me now for letting Morvé be chosen.*

Suddenly feeling sober, he stood and walked stiffly outside, to where Prince Jason and his band waited. The one in the lionskin—his name was Hercules, he remembered—was telling a rapidly growing crowd of villagers how he had killed Gryx.

"Then his teeth clamped down on my shoulder, right through my lionskin," Hercules said. He peeled back the hide, revealing a huge red mark slowly purpling. It was the worst bruise than Uram had ever seen.

"Then what did you do?" a young boy asked solemnly.

"Why, I broke his jaw!" Hercules said proudly.

Uram shook his head. Morvé had spoken truly, then. These heroes and adventurers had saved them . . . and unwittingly sentenced them to death.

Hercules got to the part where he broke the monster's neck, and as he did, everyone began to cheer. His own people seemed to be rejoicing in Gryx's death, Uram thought. But then, it had been twenty years since the myserae had descended on Thorna. They had forgotten the old horrors.

"Stop it!" he cried, stepping forward. Everyone grew silent, looking almost guilty. Prince Jason bowed his head respectfully, as did the other Argonauts. "You lied to me," Uram said accusingly.

"Witta asked us to kill Gryx," Jason said firmly. "She said it was Athena's will."

"She is not in charge here."

"We saved your children," Hercules said.

"Gryx had already devoured one boy," Atalanta added softly. "Do you feel nothing for him? For the others Gryx murdered over the years?"

"You fools," Uram hissed. He felt a blinding rage run through him. "You've saved eleven, but killed us all!"

"Gryx is dead—he will never bother you again." Hercules folded his arms across his broad chest. "You are safe now."

"But the myserae—"

Hercules snorted. "Children's tales."

Movement in the sky caught Uram's attention. He stared. A shadow moved across the sun, then another, then a third.

He sank to his knees. "May the gods spare us!" he croaked.

"What are you talking about?" Jason demanded.

Pointing at the sky, Uram whispered, "The myserae."

A hush fell over everyone as a winged shadow swept across the village. People began shading their eyes and peering up at the sky. Then, from the sun, with a rush of huge leathery wings, a black birdlike creature reached out of the sky with taloned claws, grabbed one of the Argonauts by the left shoulder and started to lift him off the ground. The man screamed in pain.

"Orpheus!" Atalanta called.

Uram shuddered, then forced himself to his feet. "Take cover!" he shouted. They stood no chance against the myserae. It was starting again, just like before. "Lock your doors! Shutter your windows! The myserae are here!"

As the giant birdlike creature grappled Orpheus and tried to carry him into the sky, Hercules leaped forward and seized one of its taloned legs. It couldn't fly with his weight too, and after a few seconds, it flapped back to land, dropping its prey.

Craning its head around, it tried to peck Hercules with its long black beak. Hercules slammed his fist against its head—once, twice, thrice—and it went limp, almost bowling him over with its weight. By all the gods, he thought, it had to be forty feet from wingtip to wingtip, and its long, sharp black beak had a wickedly hooked barb on the end. He lifted the creature and broke its back across his knee just to make sure it *was* dead and not stunned.

"Keep an eye out for others like it," Jason called, hurrying over. Everyone else hefted their spears and began to watch the sky.

Orpheus sat on the ground trying to stop the blood gushing from the punctures in his shoulder. Crouching beside him, Hercules eased his hand away from the wounds. Finger-sized holes had been poked through Orpheus's shoulder all the way to the bone. Blood welled up steadily.

"Keep pressing there," Hercules said, steering Orpheus's hand back into place. He would be lucky if he didn't get a bad infection. "We'll sew you up back on the *Argo*. Can you stand?"

"I'm better standing than flying with that thing," Orpheus said through clenched teeth. "I'll be all right."

"Can you make it back to the *Argo*?" Jason asked.

"I think so. Give me a hand up?"

Hercules pulled him to his feet. Orpheus winced a bit, but picked up his spear with his good hand and, using it for a walking stick, headed toward the beach where the *Argo* lay at anchor.

"Nalos, Iacoros, see him safely back," Jason said.

"Yes, sir!" they called, and they jogged after Orpheus.

Jason bent to examine the creature. Hercules joined him. On closer inspection, this myserae was less like a bird than Hercules had first thought. Rather than feathers, it had a black, leathery skin covered with tufts of thick, bristly hair. Its glassy red eyes were slits, like a cat's. When Jason forced its beak open, Hercules glimpsed a long, thin forked tongue. He gave a shudder. A monster like none he had ever seen before, indeed!

"There's another one!" Telamon said, pointing. Hercules leaped to his feet. Overhead, the myserae spiraled far above. It seemed to be studying them from a distance. With those slitted eyes, Hercules thought, it could see everything on the ground, even from such a height.

"And a third!" Philoran called. Hercules spotted it a moment later, circling even higher and to the left. Suddenly the pair veered sharply to the east and quickly vanished from sight.

"Scouts?" Jason wondered aloud.

"It looks that way," Hercules said.

When he turned, he found Atalanta regarding him with her hands on her hips.

"You forgot your promise," she said with mock severity.

"Oops," he said. The myserae was supposed to have been her monster to kill. "I, uh, didn't think you were up to it . . ."

"Don't worry," she said, nudging the creature with one toe. "I'll take the next *two*."

"That's a deal."

She swayed suddenly and would have fallen had he not grabbed her arm again to steady her. Clearly she hadn't fully recovered yet. So much for her fighting off monsters.

"Thanks," she said.

Hercules cleared his throat and folded his arms, looking at her expectantly.

"All right," she said, "I admit it. I *wasn't* up to killing this myserae bird. I'll just take the next monster, not two."

"Okay," he said with a laugh.

Honest as well as beautiful and brave . . . he grinned. Definitely his type of woman.

Slowly the villagers began to emerge from their houses again. They stared at the myserae's corpse with awed expressions.

"You killed it so quickly," one woman marveled.

"It wasn't hard." Hercules made a deprecating gesture. "Anyone for a feast? It would be a shame to let all this meat go to waste."

Uram stepped forward. "It is unclean," he said. "It must be burned. At once." He motioned to several villagers, and with looks of distaste, they stepped forward.

Atalanta blocked their way. "Hercules killed it," she said. "The body is his to do with as he pleases."

Everyone looked at Hercules. "Very well," he said. "Burn it."

"Aren't you even going to take a trophy?" Atalanta asked him. "A foot . . . maybe the beak?"

Hercules regarded the body silently for a moment, then shook his head.

"Not this time," he said. Uram had spoken truly. This creature *was* unclean. It needed to be burned. Let the flames purify it.

Then Atalanta paused, listening. "What's that noise?" she asked.

Hercules heard it too—a deep thrumming noise like hundreds of beating wings. He turned in time to see more myserae appearing behind them, flying low over the trees . . . not one or two, but *hundreds*.

TEN

FORM A RING!'' HERCULES SHOUTED. He waved his spear over his head, and two of the creatures veered sharply away from him, clearly looking for an easier target. By all the gods, he had never seen such a swarm, not even when locusts came.

''Run!'' Uram was shouting to his people. ''Hide until they go!''

He turned. Hercules saw him try to make it to his house and safety, but two of the creatures swooped down on him, slashing with their talons. Screaming, the elder stumbled and fell, and in seconds, a dozen more swarmed on top of his body, ripping and slashing with their beaks, sending up a fine red mist of blood.

Hercules raised his spear as Jason, Meleagar, Atalanta, Philoran, and Telamon joined him, backs to each other in a tight ring, weapons held ready. He jabbed at one of the myserae as it landed and took a tentative hop toward him, hissing. It leaped back, wings beating the air, and tried to slash him with its talons. He threw off its attack, parrying rapidly, then ran his spear through its chest.

Almost before he could wrench the bronze spearhead free, two more myserae attacked him from the air, screeching wildly. Ducking, he thrust upward and struck one creature's foot. Hissing angrily, it flew away.

For a second, Hercules was left alone. He panted, gazing around him at the carnage. Dozens of the villagers had fallen, and the myserae swarmed over their bodies like an army of ants, hacking them to pieces and devouring their flesh. To his left, Atalanta still fought one; the creature seemed to sense her injury, and it swooped at her again and again, talons out.

He hesitated for a moment, not wanting to interfere if she could kill it herself, but suddenly she collapsed with a moan.

Hercules threw his spear in a blur of motion, and it buried itself in the attacking creature's chest.

With a squawk, it tried to fly away, and after a frantic second, it plummeted to the ground. Jason leaped forward and savagely lopped the creature's head off. Blood fountained out.

Cautiously, Hercules moved forward and wrenched his spear free from the myserae's chest, feeling it grate against bone. Then he stepped back, and the other Argonauts formed a new circle around Atalanta.

No more attacks came, though. The remaining myserae seemed to be feeding voraciously. They hunched over the bodies of villagers, gorging themselves. A few squawked and hissed at each other, quarreling over some choice tidbit, but seconds later, they settled down and continued to feed.

He noticed that Maenar's body had already been stripped of most of its flesh. A pair of myserae worked at cracking open the man's bones and feasting on the marrow inside. Swallowing, he felt anger and disgust—this was no proper way to treat a hero's body—but he knew they could do little about it right now.

"Do you think they'll attack us again?" Meleagar asked Jason in a low voice.

"I don't know," Jason replied softly. "But I don't think we should wait here to find out. Hercules, can you carry Atalanta?"

"Yes." He bent and scooped her up, tossing her over one shoulder. Her head had begun to bleed again; she seemed to be unconscious. Hopefully, she would recover soon. At least none of the myserae had gotten to her.

"Back to the *Argo*," Jason said. Turning, he started up the beach at a jog, sword out and ready. The others followed.

Two hundred and fifty yards up the beach, Jason spotted movement ahead. He halted and raised one hand, squinting into the setting sun. More myserae . . . and they seemed to be clumped over a body, or bodies. His heart gave a lurch as he remembered sending Orpheus back to the ship with Telamon and Nalos. Had he sent them to their death?

"Is it them?" Hercules asked beside him.

"I don't know." Frowning, he started forward.

"Jason!" a low voice called from their right.

Jason peered into the thick underbrush. "Orpheus?" he called.

"Yes. I'm here with Telamon," Orpheus said. His voice cracked a bit with strain. "They fell on us from the sky—"

"I know," Jason said grimly, starting toward the brush. "The village is overrun with them. We were lucky to get out."

He pushed his way into a thicket and came upon Orpheus. Telamon, beside him, had been badly wounded by the myserae; he bled from a dozen gashes to his face, hands, and chest. Breath wheezed in his throat.

"They tried to protect me," Orpheus croaked. Jason turned to him, saw the fresh wounds on his face and hands, too. "When Nalos fell, they swarmed on top of him. By Apollo, it was horrible. Horrible. The blood . . . and then Telamon collapsed, and I dragged him here, and I—"

"Hush," Jason said. Orpheus was babbling from shock. "Save your strength," he said. He looked back. "Hercules?"

"I'll get him, too," Hercules said, handing his spear to Jason. In his free hand, he picked up Telamon almost gingerly, as he would a small child. He still had Atalanta slung over his shoulder.

"On to the ship," Jason said, returning to the beach and starting again for the *Argo*. He circled well around the feeding myserae, but as he half expected, they didn't even look in his direction. They were too busy gorging themselves. Nalos had clearly been dead for some time.

They continued up the beach, and at last the *Argo* came in sight, anchored fifty yards out to sea. One of the small boats had been pulled up on the sand, and there Theseus, Orestes, and half a dozen others waited with drawn weapons. Theseus and Orestes sprinted over to join them.

"Are you all right?" Orestes called.

"Maenar and Nalos are dead," Jason said. He paused and motioned for Hercules to put his burdens down. "Telamon and Atalanta are wounded. Can you see to them?"

"Stand back." Theseus gave Atalanta's head wound a quick glance, then hurried over to Telamon and began checking his wounds. After only a second's look, he began ripping the hem of Telamon's tunic and binding up the worst of the gashes in his arms and chest.

"Will he live?" Jason asked Theseus in a low voice.

"His flesh is chill," Theseus said. "He has lost a lot of blood."

"But will he live?"

"Time will tell. I'd say it's up to the gods." Theseus tied the last bandage in place, then rose. "Get him aboard the *Argo*," he said to Meleagar and Orestes. They picked up Telamon and carried him toward the boat. "I will sew up his cuts and pack them in healing herbs there," Theseus told Jason. Then he turned to Hercules and called, "Can you bring Atalanta?"

"Of course." Hercules picked her up as though she weighed little more than a feather.

She struggled, and Jason heard her mumbling something about being able to walk on her own. Hercules grinned more broadly than ever.

"That's the second time I've saved your life today," he told her, sounding almost proud. "You're slipping."

"Another monster you owe me, you mean," she countered. "Put me *down*—"

Laughing, he carried her up the beach. Jason had to smile. Their friendly competition seemed to keep them both on their toes. Then his smile soured as he remembered what the myserae had done to the village.

Turning to Theseus, he asked, "Did the myserae attack the *Argo*?"

"Yes, but that priestess—Witta—warned us of what they were the moment they flew into sight, and we took shelter in the hold. We could hear them walking on deck and scratching at the hatch, but they could not get inside and soon left."

"If Uram knew the myserae would come, then Witta must have known it, too," Jason said, musing. "And yet she did nothing to warn her own people . . . or me."

"Would you have believed her?"

Jason frowned. He *had* dismissed Uram's warnings as the prattle of an old man. They had seemed the sort of foolish tales mothers told their children to make them behave.

"Perhaps not," he admitted. "But how could Witta have known and not warned her own people? They might have been able to fight off the myserae if they had been prepared. Or they could have hidden in their houses.''

"How many died there?'' Theseus asked.

"Maybe fifty or sixty, maybe more. A lot, certainly more than Gryx would have devoured in many years.'' He suddenly understood why Uram had allowed the cyclops to eat villagers in exchange for protection. "We should not have interfered,'' he said bitterly. "They were better off before we arrived.''

"That,'' Theseus said fiercely, "is reason enough for Witta not to have warned you. I wouldn't have warned you if I knew you would spare Gryx!''

Jason frowned. "What do you mean?''

"You cannot allow one evil to continue in order to prevent a greater evil. You must stop both evils. I learned that lesson many years ago, when my father paid blood tribute to King Minos of Crete each year. It prevented war between Athens and Crete, but Athens lost the cream of her youth. King Minos used them to feed his minotaur . . . a horrible, evil death.''

"It's not the same,'' Jason protested.

"It is the same. In killing Gryx, you ended the first evil. Now you must end the second.''

"The myserae, you mean.''

Theseus nodded. "Witta says they live on an island three or four days' sail from here. She knows the course. We must go there, find their lair . . . and make sure they never plague Thorna again.''

Jason hesitated for only an instant. He knew Theseus was right. "Very well,'' he said suddenly, starting for the Argo. "Let's set sail. I won't rest until this evil is put right.''

"Good,'' Theseus said, matching his stride. "The hull has been properly caulked and braced. The ship's ready. Let's go!''

ELEVEN

ABOARD THE *ARGO*, HERCULES eased Atalanta down onto a pallet in the middle of the deck, then glanced back to shore. Jason and Theseus still stood on the beach talking. He knew they were discussing the myserae. Those monsters had to be tracked down and destroyed, just like the hydra, or the Nemean Lion, or so many other monsters he had faced and slain.

Atalanta gazed up at him. "Thank you," she said simply.

"Now I *know* you're delirious," he told her, half serious.

Witta appeared beside them and placed her hand on Atalanta's forehead. Atalanta winced.

"You have a fever," the priestess said.

"It's just a bump."

"You will recover by tomorrow," Witta pronounced.

"It is a minor wound. I will make you an herbal tonic. It will help ease the pain."

"Are you a healer as well as a priestess?" Hercules asked.

"I have some skill in the healing arts."

"You should go back to your village, then," Hercules told her. After the myserae's attack, her people would need her help. "There are many who need a healer."

"My daughter and several others also know the healing ways. They will tend to my people." Slowly, she shook her head, a dreamy, distant look in her eyes. "I must sail with you to help destroy the myserae. That is my destiny."

"How can you help?"

"First, I will finish bandaging your wounded. After that, Athena will guide me as she sees fit." Rising, she crossed to where Telamon lay and, kneeling, began pulling small packets from her bag: needle, thread, little bundles of dried leaves. Quickly she began to dress Telamon's wounds and sew the worst of them shut.

Atalanta lay back and closed her eyes. In a second, she began to snore softly.

"Let her rest," Witta said to Hercules without looking up. "It is the best thing for her."

Hercules nodded. Sleep might well be the best medicine, he thought. Rising, he turned and found himself face-to-face with Hylas. The young man twisted his hands together anxiously.

"Where is my brother?" he asked Hercules, searching his face as if for answers. "Nobody will tell me what happened."

"Come." Gently, Hercules put his arm around Hylas's shoulder and led him to the bow of the *Argo*. Hercules had lost his wife and children years ago, and he still felt that pain keenly when something—a stray word, a woman's look, a child's toy—brought back those sorrowful memories. He knew what Hylas must be going through

. . . would go through tonight. He would do his best to ease that pain now.

"Do you see that spot?" He pointed to the spit of land separating their section of the beach from the village.

"Yes," Hylas said.

"Your brother fought off twenty myserae as long as he could," Hercules said gently. It was only a slight exaggeration. Better for him to have died as valiantly as possible. "When Telamon fell, your brother fought on, giving Orpheus time to drag Telamon into the underbrush. It was a true hero's death. We will drink to him tonight."

Hylas's shoulders slumped, and Hercules saw a shudder run through him.

"Was he your only family?" Hercules asked softly.

Hylas nodded.

"Weep for him," Hercules said, "but keep his memory alive. Never forget him."

"I won't." Hylas took several gulps of air. "I won't."

Hercules hesitated, then put his arm around the young man's shoulders again. "We are your family now," he said gently. "All of us aboard the *Argo*. We have all lost friends and loved ones. If there is anything we can do . . . anything *I* can do . . ."

Suddenly Hylas broke away from him and ran down the deck, climbed through an open hatch and disappeared from sight. Hercules sighed heavily. His own son would have been about Hylas's age now.

He bit his lip and turned to look back out toward the beach. Jason and Theseus had climbed aboard the boat; Meleagar and Laertes rowed them strongly toward the *Argo*.

He would keep an eye on Hylas, he told himself. Perhaps, when they returned from this voyage, he would adopt him as his son. He needed an heir. It might be nice to settle down, marry again, raise a family. Perhaps Atalanta—

Then he shook his head. No, he could never marry.

Hera had destroyed everyone and everything he had ever loved. He would not risk it again.

Taking a deep, cleansing breath, he watched Witta as she worked, hands sure and certain as she finished stitching up Telamon's wounds, then moved on to Orpheus. These myserae would die, he vowed. An anger smoldering within him burst to flames. Nothing would stop him from destroying them once and for all.

Hercules found his impatience growing over the next few days. They sailed east, and the weather remained fair, with a strong, favorable breeze. If the gods had tried to destroy them before, then surely they blessed them now . . . or, he thought bleakly, they knew what kind of doom awaited the Argonauts when they found the myserae again.

Their visit on Thorna seemed to be weighing heavily on everyone, he reflected. Witta hid in her cabin. Hylas remained sullen and barely responsive as the shock of his loss settled in. Atalanta recovered, as predicted, but her mood seemed dark, almost somber. Telamon slowly began to regain his strength.

The rest of the crew seemed much the same. None of them looked forward to fighting the myserae—none except Theseus, he decided after a moment's thought, and perhaps Hylas. Theseus seemed to be spending all of his time talking to Witta and Jason about the best strategies to use against the creatures. Hylas seemed perpetually on lookout duty, scanning the skies for the abominations and the horizon for their island.

On the third day out from Thorna, Hercules wandered onto deck at dawn and spotted Theseus and Jason in the bow. They were staring silently off at the horizon when he joined them.

"Any sign of them?" he asked.

"A few gulls," Jason said. "That's it."

Hercules gave a sigh. "It's big, the sea. We could have missed the isle."

"If so, we'll circle around and try again," Theseus said.

"*Land!*" the lookout called from above. "*Land to starboard!*"

Hercules turned and squinted, but he couldn't see more than a faint gray smudge—little more than a shadow—far off on the horizon. It looked like clouds to him.

"What do you think?" Theseus asked Jason.

"If that's not the myserae's island, maybe the people there know where it is."

"Good idea," Hercules said. "Shall I wake everyone and have them prepare for battle?" He stretched his powerful muscles. It would be good to be off the ship and moving again.

"Not yet," Jason said. "We're several hours out yet. Let them sleep while they can." Then he headed aft, calling orders. The *Argo* shifted course to starboard, heading for land.

Three hours later, most of the crew stood on deck, weapons out and ready. Once land had been sighted, nothing could keep them below. Hercules felt the same way: a pressing need to be ashore, hunting the monsters, making them pay for the evil they had done.

The island had inhabitants, he saw as they drew near. A ridge of mountains ran its length, and what appeared to be thick forests grew along their sides. However, he saw on the eastern end what could only be a walled city. It surrounded a natural harbor. To either side there spread a patchwork of fields and carefully planted orchards.

Even though they were still half an hour out from land, he found himself pacing impatiently. Finally he stalked forward and joined Jason in the bow.

"What do you think?" he asked.

"The fields look too well tended. And there seem to

be boats in the harbor. To all appearances, it's a prosperous city," Jason replied.

Hercules squinted as a bright light suddenly winked at them from the city's wall. A mirror—someone was signaling.

"This can't be the right island," Jason muttered to himself. "How could anyone live here alongside the myserae?"

"They may know how to protect themselves," Hercules said. "The only way to find out is to put ashore." He turned and called to Hylas, "Find a mirror!"

"A mirror?" Hylas echoed. "Where?"

"Ask Atalanta. She ought to have one," Hercules said.

"Well, I don't!" Atalanta called back. "I'm not that rich! Find someone rich and vain."

Hercules glanced at Jason and raised his eyebrows. "Rich?"

Jason patted the railing. "My meager fortune is tied up in the *Argo*. When I'm king, maybe then . . ."

"Does *anyone* have a mirror?" Hercules called.

The rest of the Argonauts muttered among themselves and looked from one to another. Several voices called, "No!"

"I'll just have to use my sword," Jason said. He drew it and turned the bronze blade to the sun, flashing once, twice, thrice to the people on the city walls.

They flashed back; then abruptly their mirror vanished. *They're probably on the way to the docks to meet us*, Hercules thought.

The wind died as the *Argo* approached shore. He estimated that at the ship's present speed, they would reach the docks in another hour or so—certainly long enough for the local king to prepare a fitting reception. And since there were no great masses of wealth to attract pirates to these waters, the townsfolk would be expecting traders, or perhaps visitors from one of the neighboring islands. It would be nice to have a proper reception.

"This is the island," a woman's low voice said behind them.

Hercules and Jason both turned. Witta stood there, her eyes dark and strange as she gazed toward the shore. Her age-lined face was set with determination, and her long white hair fluttered loose in the breeze.

"How do you know?" Jason demanded. "Have you been here before?"

"No . . ." She hesitated. "It is a feeling I have."

"Then why are there so many people here?" Jason asked her. "Why haven't the myserae attacked them, like they attacked your people?

"I do not know," she admitted. "It is a mystery."

When they finally reached the city's docks, they saw that a festival seemed to have sprung up, almost as an afterthought. Jason studied the bright red and green banners fluttering from the city's wall, the gaily dressed people clustered on the dock, and farther back on the beach, all the commoners who had turned out to watch and cheer.

The *Argo* drifted to the left side of the main dock, nosing in among small fishing boats. The Argonauts slacked the sails and dragged out the mooring lines, preparing to tie up the ship.

Hercules stood in the prow, feet braced on the railings, grasping the fo'c'sle's taut rope in his right hand to keep his balance. He smiled, eager, impatient, as was his wont. Jason wondered for a second if that impatience would get them into trouble here. Hercules always seemed to be chasing trouble, trying to right every wrong and slay every monster in the world. They had a mission here, and they could not afford to be sidetracked, as they had been on the mainland when Hercules led a handful of people off to slay a sea-monster menacing Troy.

As the *Argo* bumped up against the dock, a small delegation moved forward: three men, one young and richly dressed in opulent white and purple robes, a circlet of gold on his head; the other two older, bearded, more sedate in mien and manner. Hercules guessed the young one to be ruler of this island, and the elder two, his counselors.

Jason leaped across to the dock and with a bow to the young king, said, "Sir, I am Prince Jason of Thessaly."

The king bowed back. "I am pleased to welcome you to Sattis, Prince Jason. I am King Muros, and these are my advisors, Keros and Huron. Welcome to our humble shores. Seldom do we have visitors from so far away. Will you and your men join us for dinner tonight? I would like to hear what brings you so far from home."

"Gladly," Jason said. "Your hospitality is most welcome, Your Highness."

"And gladly shall you have it, Prince Jason," the young king replied.

Jason nodded to his crew, and mooring lines were quickly dropped and fenders lowered as the ship bumped against the dock's pilings. After swinging up a small section of railing, Orestes and Meleagar manhandled the gangplank into position, sliding home the bolts that held it secure. When they stepped back, Theseus, Hercules, and Atalanta led the way down to the dock. They bowed to King Muros, and introductions were quickly made.

"Hercules . . ." the king said softly. "I have heard that name before, I think. You have the look of a great warrior, and you must wear that lionskin for a reason. Tell me, are many tales sung of your adventures?"

"A few," Hercules said modestly. "There are many great heroes in this company. We have all joined Prince Jason for an epic quest."

King Muros seemed delighted. "I must hear of your adventures tonight," he said.

The older man to Muros's right cleared his throat.

"Ah, yes, I forget my manners, as Keros reminds me." King Muros stepped back and indicated the path toward the city. "Let us gather inside, where the air is less oppressive. You and your men can rest and refresh yourselves. I will hear your tales tonight after dinner, which is the proper time for such things."

"Of course," Jason said with another bow.

"This way," King Muros said. He turned and his advisors fell in step behind him, leaving Jason and his crew to follow.

Jason said, "Theseus, Atalanta, and Hercules—join me now. Everyone else remains here. Keep your weapons ready and watch for the myserae. We will send for you in time for the banquet."

Turning, Jason followed King Muros up the steep, winding path to the city. Along the way, he kept glancing at the sky, half expecting the myserae to appear.

After passing through the city gates, their procession reached a small compound with thick, high stone walls. All the buildings within had been painted with colorful red-and-black geometric patterns. This must be the palace, Jason thought. They walked through an archway carved in the shape of a lion and into a smaller courtyard. Here a fountain burbled happily, spewing water from a natural cleft in the rock.

"I am certain you want to refresh yourselves," King Muros said. He motioned a middle-aged man over. "This is Ieron, my chief steward. He will see to your needs."

"Thank you, Your Highness," Jason said.

King Muros nodded graciously, then led his advisors off through a side door. Jason looked to the steward.

Ieron bowed low, then led them through a different section of the palace, to a suite of rooms. Jason nodded as he studied the large but plainly furnished chambers: low couches, featherbeds, alcoves where small oil lamps sat awaiting nightfall. The high-beamed ceilings and white-washed walls gave the impression of open space. Yes, he thought, this would do quite nicely.

"I will have wine and refreshments brought," Ieron promised. "I will see that your crew receives it, too."

"Thank you," Jason said.

The steward bowed again and left.

Immediately Hercules threw himself down on the feath-erbed in his bedchamber. The wooden frame creaked as if in alarm.

"Too soft!" he called through the open door.

"You were grumbling the other day about how hard the ship's deck was," Atalanta chided him gently. "You can always go back and sleep there."

"What, and deprive you of my wit and company?"

"You're never happy," Jason told him with a grin. Those two will never change, he thought. Crossing to the window, he looked out. He could see a small courtyard just below, full of colorful pink-and-white flowers, but little else; these guest rooms seemed to have been de-signed for privacy. "But then," he went on, "none of us is ever happy. That's why we like adventure."

"Oh, you'd settle down soon enough given half a chance," Hercules said. "You *want* to be a king."

Jason laughed. "True enough."

Theseus joined him at the window, bending close. "The walls have ears," he whispered. "Say nothing of any import unless you want King Muros to know it too."

Jason gave him a puzzled glance, but nodded. Then he followed Theseus's gaze to a small clay tube set in one corner of the floor. He had taken it as a drain of some kind, but now he realized the floor sloped ever so slightly *away* from it. A listening tube? It had to be.

Theseus circled the room, warning first Atalanta, then Hercules. Their banter stopped abruptly. Jason quickly motioned for them to continue, though, and Hercules nod-ded: they had to keep up the pretense of ignorance.

"You know," Hercules said, as if he had paused for a second to think, "these people seem just as nice as the Trojans. I know we'll enjoy ourselves tonight."

"Oh, you'd enjoy yourself anywhere," Atalanta said lightly. "Do you remember the first time we met?"

"You were a mere child!" Hercules said. "You had your hair in a ponytail down your back, almost to your waist, I believe—"

"Met properly, I meant. I was fifteen, and in charge of a boar hunt—"

"Oh, yes, I do recall that."

And so their conversation continued on an innocent note, as if they had nothing in the world to hide.

Jason exchanged another look with Theseus. His opinion of King Muros had gone down a few notches. Hosts did not spy on the guests . . . or eavesdrop on private conversations. It did not bode well for the future, he thought uneasily. Then he turned his gaze upward, to the sky. And what of the myserae?

King Muros slipped the stone back into the wall, covering the listening tube. This room sat directly below Jason's, although the entrances were on opposite sides of the building.

"They're not going to say anything," he said with a sigh. "They're talking about things that happened years ago."

As his counselors pondered the matter, the chamberlain shuffled in and began laying out clothes for dinner that night: a fine white-linen tunic with intricate patterns in gold and silver threads, gold-and-silver slippers, and various rings and signets. He seemed to be moving more slowly than usual, King Muros thought. Probably listening to their plans.

He cleared his throat and, half joking, turned to the chamberlain. "Well, Vargas, since you're so interested, what would *you* do?" It wasn't the first time he'd played this game with the old man. Whenever anything interesting happened, Vargas always seemed to offer his opinion.

The chamberlain finished smoothing the tunic, then straightened. "My thoughts, Highness? Why, I think it's obvious. You should kill them and take their ship."

"And then what would I do with it?"

"Sail your own traders to Mycenae, or Sparta, or Troy, or wherever you wish, Highness."

Muros caught his breath. He could see what Vargas suggested: himself standing in the front end of the ship, feet braced on the rails, gazing heroically off to the left. Around him the crackling of sails, the lap of waves . . .

"Yes!" he whispered. It was a direct, unexpected blow, the sort of thing that only a servant would have the lack of subtlety necessary to think up. But first he would find out why they had come. After dinner, that would be the time to strike. They would be sated with food. No, even better, he would get them to order all their men ashore for a feast in their honor. . . .

TWELVE

HERCULES LEANED BACK IN HIS seat, full with rich food and light-headed with wine. King Muros had a good life here, he thought as he listened to the buzz of talk and gazed at the people around him.

Large but comfortable, the palace banquet hall had a high, arched ceiling with rows of polished wooden pillars to either side. Oil lamps burned at the sides, spreading a pleasant yellow glow. Several dozen people—petty nobility from the island—sat with him at the main table. The women wore long, shimmering gowns, their hair was elegantly coiffed, gold rings shone on their hands, and intricate broaches gleamed at their throats. All the men were dressed in embroidered white tunics.

A servant offered him more roast lamb braised in honey, but he waved the platter away. He didn't think he could eat another bite.

In all, ten long tables had been set up for the feast in

their honor. Theseus and Atalanta sat next to him. At the main table, to the king's right and in the place of honor reserved for special guests, sat Jason. Hercules couldn't hear what they were saying, but it seemed to amuse Muros; the king threw back his head and laughed heartily several times. The twenty other crewmen Jason had brought to the feast sat among the other tables with lesser members of the court.

Jason had cautioned everyone not to mention the myserae or their true purpose in visiting Sattis. He wanted to bring it up himself, and Hercules agreed with that plan. For some reason, he felt distinctly uneasy about King Muros. It probably had to do with the listening tube that Theseus had discovered in their room. That, and the fact that Witta insisted the myserae came from this island, though they saw no sign of them.

Finally, King Muros stood. The room fell silent.

"A toast to our guests!" the king cried, raising his wine bowl. All his people echoed his words, and they drank.

Now it was Jason's turn, and he returned the toast. Hercules drank heartily, then wiped his mouth on the back of his arm. Good food and good wine, he thought, made for a grand celebration.

"Tell me, Prince Jason—" King Muros said as musicians began strolling around the room playing soft melodies on lyres and hand drums. Talk resumed at the other tables, but Hercules noticed that everyone around him had turned to watch Jason and the king. "—what news is there of Athens and the other great states of Greece?"

Jason straightened. "The usual. Kings squabble and make treaties. Wars are threatened, then the threats are quickly forgotten as new treaties are made. There has been peace for nearly ten years now."

"Your ship is most impressive. Are there many like it?"

"No, it was built for me by Argos, the greatest shipbuilder in Greece. I imagine he will make more in time.

I can see a fleet of them traveling the world, trading with hundreds of kingdoms, in twenty or thirty years.''

Muros nodded and took a sip of his wine. "I would welcome more contact with you and your people. Perhaps even regular trade in time. We may be far apart, but I'm sure we have much to offer each other. This wine, for instance." He held up his bowl.

"An excellent vintage," Jason said, and Hercules found himself murmuring in agreement, along with half the table.

"It is a simple summer wine," King Muros said, "from my own vineyards on the north side of the island. And yet those outlanders who taste it swear it is exceptional. Perhaps you could arrange a trading mission after your return from this quest?"

"I am only a prince, not the king of Thessaly," Jason said, "and I'm afraid my opinion carries little weight back home right now." And then he launched into a brief version of his family history, including the fact that his uncle refused to give up the throne that was rightfully Jason's.

Muros nodded, his attention rapt. When Jason came to the part about gathering all the heroes of Greece for an epic quest for the Golden Fleece, hoping to shame his uncle into surrendering the throne peacefully, Muros sighed enviously, a far-off look in his eyes.

"I wish I could join you," he finally said. "Unfortunately, my people need me here. How long can I persuade you to stay?"

"Not too much longer, alas." Jason said. "We have a long voyage ahead of us, and there are many dangers we have yet to face."

"I can imagine. Is there anything I can do to help you?"

"Well . . ." Jason seemed to hesitate. This would be his chance to bring up the myserae, Hercules thought.

"Tell me, please," Muros urged.

"I have heard rumors of monsters inhabiting these islands," Jason said cautiously.

"Monsters?" The king laughed. "There are no monsters here."

"Your Highness," Jason said, "the warning was quite specific. We were told to steer clear of the island where the myserae dwell. This island, in fact."

"What are these myserae?" Muros asked with a frown. "I have never heard of them."

"They are like birds," Hercules said, "but huge, with leathery wings and talons sharp enough to rip through armor."

"That sounds like a tale told to frighten children," Muros said. He made a dismissive gesture. "I have never seen such a creature, thank the gods! No, you are certainly safe here from any of these myserae."

When Jason nodded, Hercules chewed his lip in puzzlement. He might not like or particularly trust King Muros, but something told him that their host told the truth: he really *hadn't* heard of the myserae before. Could Witta have been wrong?

"I had planned a hunt for tomorrow," Muros said. "Will you and your most able hunters join me?"

"We would be honored," Jason said. "Hercules, Theseus, and Atalanta will join us, with your permission."

Muros inclined his head. "And tomorrow night," he said, "I will give a farewell banquet for the rest of your people. We will make it a festival for the whole island! I'll have my cooks prepare the game we find. We will roast it all on the beach."

"A brilliant idea," Jason said. "My Argonauts are undoubtedly tired from the trip—I know *I* am—and we can all use the chance to stretch our legs ashore. You have no idea of how uncomfortable sea travel can be."

"Oh?" said King Muros with a strange intensity. "Tell me about it."

Jason did, in great detail, from the roiling of storms to

the broiling heat of summer when the winds died away. And then their talk drifted on to different things. A dozen new conversations started around them as the meal resumed. A few men joked about the myserae, Hercules noticed. These people truly *hadn't* heard of the creatures, he thought in surprise.

Then the king called on Hercules for the tale of the lionskin he wore. Hercules launched into the telling of his famous Twelve Tasks and how he had defeated the Nemean Lion, whose skin could not be pierced by any weapons, by wrestling it to the ground and strangling it with his bare hands.

"But that happened long ago," he said. He gave Atalanta a sly glance. "You must ask Atalanta here for the tale of the Trojan sea-monster, which she slew only a week ago!"

"Oh?" said the young king, eyebrows raised. He looked to Atalanta. "Please, I must hear this story, too!"

Hercules half expected Atalanta to laugh and make light of the request, but she took the bait and rose. "It was dawn when we first saw the monster," she said, and she recounted the adventure with gusto, embellishing here and there, adding spice and mystery. She actually told it quite well, Hercules thought as he found himself listening eagerly, even though he knew the outcome.

"Why would he lie?" King Muros wondered aloud.

After the banquet, he and his counselors retired to the palace library. He crossed the room and sat down at an ancient, scarred oak table. Pushing aside a stack of clay tablets, he spread open a leather map of the Mediterranean Sea. Many places had little more than sketchy lines, but the heart of Greece, yes . . . there all the kingdoms had been clearly drawn in.

He found Thessaly quickly enough. It lay four hundred miles away, far enough to be a risky voyage even under the best of conditions. Leaning back, he pondered Jason's story.

A prince questing for some mythical Golden Fleece, indeed! He had never heard such an implausible story. And what of these myserae . . . leather-winged, birdlike monsters no one had ever seen or heard of before. No, there had to be another reason for their visit to Sattis. What was it?

"Why have they *really* come here?" he asked.

Keros stroked his thin gray beard. "Obviously, Prince Jason has plans to conquer an empire," he said. "Why else would he sail with so many great warriors?"

"And," Huron added, "you will be dragged through the streets in chains. That's what they do to conquered kings. And your head and hands will be chopped off in a public execution, then hung atop the city gates."

Muros shook his head grimly. It was not a fate he looked forward to. "Then we must make sure his ship doesn't make it back to Thessaly."

"A pity," Keros said. "I almost like Jason. Were he an honorable man, I would welcome trade with his people."

"But that Hercules . . ." Huron said with a shiver. "A savage!"

On that, they all agreed. They began to count the available members of the city guard, planning where to station them during the festival on the beach, and to discuss what to do with the Argonauts they captured.

Jason and Hercules, the king decided, would both be put to death at once.

After the banquet, Jason lay in bed uneasily. True, King Muros had been the perfect host at dinner, but something was wrong and he couldn't quite put his finger on it. He heard soft breathing and snores from everyone else's rooms and knew they were asleep; well, it was the leader's job to do the worrying for all, he told himself.

The listening tube continued to trouble him. What if King Muros *did* intend some sort of treachery? What if he planned to try to steal the *Argo*? It had happened before; such a magnificent vessel made a very tempting target.

Suddenly he decided he had to do something. He couldn't just lie here and brood on the dangers around them. They had to protect themselves and their ship . . . and that meant taking precautions now, when he knew he could make them without arousing any of the king's suspicions. Tomorrow might well be too busy, with the morning's hunt and then the evening's feast on the beach.

Rising, he dressed quickly. He needed to see Orestes, he decided. He eased open the door and looked up and down the corridor. Frescoes showing familiar scenes of the gods and the legends surrounding them had been painted on the walls, and an intricate mosaic of dancers covered the floor. At the far end of the hall, near the wide stairs that wound down to the audience chamber, a pair of men in leather armor stood watch. Their polished bronze speartips gleamed faintly even in the dim light. They saw him and straightened, so he stepped out.

"Ah, good," he said loudly. "Perhaps one of you can show me the way back to my ship?"

"Certainly, sir," the one on the right said. He was short, but strongly built. He stepped back and indicated the stairs. "This way."

They went down through the entrance hall, out into the courtyard, through a small side gate, and down a winding path by the city's wall. The night was dark, with only the faintest sliver of moon showing, and Jason had a little trouble seeing his way. He stumbled once on a rock and nearly fell. The guard paused and waited in silence. Jason moved forward more cautiously after that. Already he could smell brine on the wind.

Suddenly he felt sand crunching under his sandals; the docks stood a hundred yards to the left. The *Argo* looked unchanged. The ship rolled a bit with low swells from an incoming tide, and he could hear the soft slap of waves against the hull. A few oil lamps hung in the rigging, spreading a soft glow across the decks, where he could see his men lounging. About half seemed to be asleep. In the stern, Orestes was playing a harp and singing.

"Will you be coming back up to the city this night?" the guard asked suddenly.

"Yes," Jason said.

"Very well. I will wait for you."

"I shouldn't be long," Jason said, and he continued alone, breathing more easily. He had thought the guard might be bold enough to try to follow him aboard the *Argo*, and he wanted to talk to his men alone right now.

The man on watch had seen him and called to the others. Everyone still awake hurried to greet him.

"Any news of the myserae?" several people called.

"Not yet," Jason replied. He had left Orestes in charge, and he motioned for him to join him in his cabin.

Inside, Jason paced, thinking of all King Muros had said. At last he spoke: "The people here seem honest enough, but something about them makes me distinctly uneasy. I'm supposed to join Muros for a hunt tomorrow, and for the evening, he plans a banquet on the beach in our honor. He wants everyone to attend."

"I heard about that from some of the servants who brought us food tonight," Orestes said. "Could it be a trap, sir? That would be the time to strike."

Jason shrugged. "I don't know. I'm not sure, but I want to be ready for anything. Since Muros will doubtless keep me busy tomorrow, I may not get to see you before the feast. I want you to make sure there's a skeleton crew left on the ship—a *well-armed* skeleton crew—and that all who go ashore are carrying knives and swords hidden under their clothing. And they're not to drink much. There's nothing more useless in a fight than a drunken soldier."

"Yes, sir," said Orestes. "And we'll have the ship ready to leave at a moment's notice. If necessary."

Jason smiled. "You've got it."

A knock sounded on the hatch. "Come in," Jason called.

Witta stepped inside. Tonight she had dressed all in black, with a thin veil across her face. Her eyes, dark and inscrutable, locked with his.

"Sir?" Orestes said.

"Leave us. That will be all for now."

"Yes, sir." He gave a nod and left them alone.

After the hatch had closed, Jason turned to the priestess. She seemed to be smiling, as though she knew everything he'd said to Orestes and approved. He felt a little reassured.

"The myserae *are* here, somewhere," she said. "I dreamed about them tonight, before you came."

Jason frowned. "I have seen no sign of them. And when I asked King Muros, he claimed never to have heard of the myserae. I don't think he was lying."

"Nevertheless . . ." She paused. "I also dreamed of a priest of Hera—a tall, thin man with hair as white as snow. Be careful, for I scent magic about him. He is dangerous."

"I haven't come this far to get myself killed," Jason told her.

"No," she said. "You came to save my people."

Jason found he had no answer. The storm that had washed them up on Thorna's beach *could* have been deliberately sent by one of the gods, he realized. It *could* have been Athena . . . but would the goddess do all this just to free Witta and her people from the myserae?

He did not like to think of himself as a pawn in such an epic game. But if it *was* a game, wouldn't Athena be playing against another god . . . or perhaps against a goddess, such as Hera?

THIRTEEN

WHEN HERCULES AWAKENED AN hour before dawn, he found breakfast waiting. Servants had carried in silver trays heaped with apples and figs, fresh warm bread, hard-boiled eggs, and cold roast pheasant while he slept. It all smelled delicious. After helping himself to a pheasant, he sat down next to Atalanta.

"What kind of game do you think lives on this island?" she asked, pouring him a bowl of red wine.

"Deer. Boar. Maybe bears." He shrugged, biting into the pheasant's leg. It was pleasantly gamy and had been spiced to perfection. "The bigger and meaner, the better!"

She laughed, then gave a pointed glance toward the listening tube in the corner. Hercules nodded; there might be other listeners. He hadn't forgotten.

Jason pushed back from the table, wiping his mouth.

"Enough talk about this hunt. Let's see what sport our gracious host has to offer!"

Hercules grabbed a small loaf of bread and followed Jason out the door, still chewing.

As dawn broke, Hercules clicked and slapped the reins against the flanks of his two horses. They stepped forward smartly, pulling his chariot through the city's west gate and onto a broad dirt road. They followed close to Jason's chariot, in which Theseus also rode.

"A little bumpy!" Atalanta said beside Hercules, her voice barely audible over the clatter of the wooden wheels as they hit the first of many deep ruts.

"It beats walking!" he shouted. Glancing over his shoulder, he estimated the rest of their hunting party at thirty-five or forty people, most of them servants. They were all on foot, and dust from the two chariots had already begun to settle on their clothes and faces. It would be a long, dry trip for them, Hercules thought.

Turning, he clicked to the horses again, trying to steer around the worst of the ruts. Ahead of their two chariots, King Muros and a dozen of his friends and relatives rode handsome, long-legged Caucasian horses, their necks decorated with jingling bells and intricately braided ropes with tassels.

They quickly left the city behind, heading north, toward the mountains, and as Hercules gazed at the lands around him, he had to admire them: rich vineyards, orchards laden with fruit, fields where the rye and oats grew tall and golden in the sun. Even the sheep, goats, and cattle grazing in the pastures looked sleek and well fed. If the myserae truly came from Sattis, they certainly paid no attention to anyone or anything living on the island, he thought.

King Muros led them away from the cultivated lands to a wild, forested valley between two of the mountains. Here game seemed plentiful; Hercules glimpsed hares darting away in the grass beside the road, and several times they came upon the spoor of deer. The road narrowed, becoming wild and half overgrown. Apparently few people came this way.

At last they arrived at a wide, grassy clearing where several billowing red-and-white-striped canopies had been set up. Tables and benches sat beneath them in the shade, and servants in spotless white tunics waited close at hand with bowls and amphorae of wine.

The king and the others on horseback dismounted, handing their reins to various waiting stable boys who led the steeds off somewhere beyond the canopies—probably to be rubbed down, then watered at some nearby stream, Hercules thought. As he drew up beside Jason's chariot, more boys stepped up to take charge of their horses, too.

"You certainly are well prepared," Jason said to the king.

Muros grinned at him. "We *have* been planning this hunt for several weeks," he said. "Luckily, you arrived in time to join us. Let's have a toast, then we'll get to it!"

He turned and led the way into the shade of the largest canopy. Picking up a drinking bowl, Muros raised it and proclaimed: "A toast to the day—may the gods grant us all success!"

Hercules echoed the king's words along with Jason and everyone else, then drained his own bowl, smacking his lips in satisfaction. Another good wine, a little heavier than the summer wine Muros had served the night before, but just as delicious.

Muros led the way over to where racks of weapons had been assembled. The king picked a bow and quiver of arrows, as did several of his men; others took spears. Jason took a brace of spears, too. Then Hercules chose three well-balanced oak shafts tipped with wide, long bronze tips, excellent for throwing or thrusting. Atalanta had brought her own bow and a quiver of arrows. Lastly,

Theseus took a set of spears like the ones Hercules had selected.

Muros scanned the crowd of hunters. "Eleven of us," he said. "I suggest we split up. Jason, would you accompany Hetton and me? And I think your man Theseus would do well to join Aramon and Lycor." Then Muros hesitated. Only five people were left, Hercules saw. Clearly the king didn't know how to pair them up.

"With your permission, Highness," Hercules said suddenly, "Atalanta and I will hunt together. We make a good team." If the king agreed, it would give the two of them a chance to look for any sign of the myserae.

"Very well," Muros said, nodding, obviously satisfied. "That leaves Oleon, Irax, and Vulmor. Let's go!"

They drew lots for quarters of the valley. The king's party won the center land—almost flat, threaded by a stream: clearly the choicest spot, Hercules knew. Muros seemed delighted. Theseus's group took the second best, the far end of the valley. Hercules chose third and got the left side, where the mountain sloped down through the thick trees.

"Tough luck," Muros told him. "A bear lives in a cave on that slope. It keeps away all but the small game."

Hercules shrugged. "We'll make do," he said.

The last group got the mountain's right slope. They seemed resigned to small game, or maybe a stray deer.

Each team called for four bearers, and then they jogged off into the trees. Hercules and Atalanta lingered until last.

"Don't you want bearers?" the hunting steward, a stout man with a bristly red beard, asked.

"Oh . . . eight should do nicely," Hercules said offhandedly. That was twice as many as anyone else had taken.

The steward seemed to be trying to hide a smirk. "Feeling lucky today?"

"If you think only four of your men can carry a whole bear . . ." Hercules replied.

The steward paled. "Do not go after that bear," he said. "It stands twelve feet high, and its claws are like knives. Six men have already died trying to kill it."

"Sounds tough," Hercules said, looking at Atalanta. "Are you up to it?"

"You promised the next monster to me," she said.

"Oh, that's no fun on a hunt! How about just the first two shots today, and you can have that monster later?"

"Fair enough." They shook hands.

The hunting steward looked from one to the other and back again. "You're crazy!" he said. "I won't risk my boys on a foolhardy stunt that's going to get them killed!"

"Suit yourself." Shouldering his spears, Hercules turned and led the way into the trees, heading toward the territory they had drawn.

It didn't take long to find signs of the bear, Atalanta quickly discovered. Hundred-pound boulders had been overturned where it had searched for rodents to eat. Huge gouges scarred trees where it had sharpened its claws repeatedly. She stared at the height of those marks. The steward had been wrong, she realized—this creature had to be at least fifteen feet tall, maybe taller, when it stood on its hind legs.

Taking a deep breath, she strung her bow and drew out a hunting arrow. No sense getting caught unprepared, she thought. They might round a bend and come face-to-face with the creature any second. Luckily, she had Hercules to back her up. She never would have dared take on a challenge such as this one without someone like him close at hand . . . though she knew she never would have admitted it to anyone.

She glanced over at her friend, in his lionskin, with three spears slung across his broad, deeply muscled shoulders. Hercules seemed almost casual about the hunt. They might have been out looking for ducks, for all the concern he showed.

"It's not much farther," he said suddenly, drawing up short.

"Do you see it?"

"Not yet. But look." He nodded to the left, where half a dozen deer had suddenly bolted into sight. They passed by not fifteen feet away, then disappeared into the undergrowth. Something big had certainly spooked them, Atalanta thought. Something *very* big. Slowly she leveled her bow, studying the trees and bushes around her. A hush had fallen over the land. Not a bird, not a squirrel, not a chipmunk made a sound.

Thirty yards away, a bush rustled. Then just as suddenly as the deer had appeared, a large brown bear pushed out into the open. It blinked slowly, as if half asleep, then threw back its head and roared. The bushes continued to rustle and a second bear, even bigger than the first, appeared.

"We're in luck," Hercules whispered.

Atalanta gulped. *Two.* She hadn't figured on *two.*

"One for each of us," Hercules continued softly. "You can have the big one this time." Calmly, he unshouldered his spears.

"Thanks," Atalanta said. Every shot would have to count, she knew. She might get off one arrow, maybe two, before the bears realized they were in danger and attacked.

She raised her bow and began to take careful aim.

Beside her, Hercules threw his first spear, hitting the bear on the left in the shoulder. Wailing, it reared, batting at the shaft with one paw. Wood splintered, but the bronze tip remained deeply buried in muscle and bone; Atalanta glimpsed bright-crimson blood on the paw.

She shot her first arrow at the larger bear, which was staring at its companion as if puzzled. Unfortunately, her hand must have shaken ever so slightly; her arrow whizzed past its head a handbreadth away. Instantly it whirled to face her, dropping onto all four paws. Throwing back its head, it snarled.

Hercules threw a second spear, hitting his bear in the chest. It made a muffled whimper and staggered a bit. His third throw came a split second later, hitting it in the throat, and then it collapsed, huge paws twitching faintly.

Atalanta swallowed. The bigger bear roared again, then lowered its head and charged her.

Stay calm, she told herself. *Take aim before you fire.* It was a lesson that had been drilled into her through years of practice. *Still your heart, still your breathing. Nothing matters but finding the perfect target, then hitting it.*

Her vision narrowed to the bear's head. The behemoth was running at her, fangs bared, drool streaming from the corners of its mouth.

Find the perfect target.

She focused on its right eye.

Take the perfect shot.

She had it. She knew it the second she released the string and the arrow began to fly.

The bear's head went down with its stride. Its rear legs touched the ground, then its front legs. Its head began to swing up.

And her arrow took it in the right eye, burying itself halfway into its skull. It collapsed, chest hitting the ground, then head, and then it did a complete flip, paws flailing, claws slashing at the air.

Strong hands shoved her to the side, and the bear landed on its back where she had been standing. The arrow had broken off; a half inch of wood protruded from the creature's eye socket, and a clear liquid, laced with blood, seeped out. But otherwise, the bear looked completely unharmed.

"Amazing," Hercules said softly.

"That shot?" She turned proudly. It *had* been extraordinary, even by her standards.

"No, that you missed the whole bear the first time!"

Then he laughed when she made a sour face. "*Of course* that shot! It was brilliant, one of the best I've ever seen."

"Truly?" she asked, a little mollified.

"Truly." He retrieved his two intact spears from the smaller bear and then wiped them clean on the grass. "Now," he went on, "I'm going to climb this mountain and see what I can find."

"The myserae," she guessed.

"If they're on the other side of the island, I'll be able to see them."

"Right." She looked up the steep, steep slope of the mountain to its snowcapped crown. It would take hours for a normal man to climb that height, she realized, maybe days. Luckily, Hercules was a demigod, with the strength of twenty men. He would need it, she thought, before this day was out. Especially if he did run into the myserae.

"What about me?" she asked. "I know I'd only slow you down."

He hesitated, and she saw he didn't want to exclude her. "Why don't you wait for a couple of hours, then go back and get the bearers?" he finally said. "That way, we won't arouse the king's suspicions. He'll think I stayed behind to protect our kills. I'll be back before the others get here."

"Agreed," she said quickly. It seemed like a good plan.

Hercules started off through the trees at a jog. Suddenly she noticed he hadn't taken his weapons.

"Wait!" she shouted. "Your spears—!"

"They would only slow me down!" he called.

Then she lost sight of him. A few minutes later, he reappeared a hundred yards up the slope, running between the trees, heading up the mountain as fast and surefooted as a goat. At that speed, he would be up the mountain in an hour, she guessed . . . maybe less.

FOURTEEN

HERCULES ALLOWED NOTHING TO slow him down. Though the mountain looked steep, small animal trails twisted this way and that up the rocky slope, and he followed them whenever possible. He also took every shortcut, scrambled up every ravine, and climbed every cliff he came to without a second's pause.

Soon he reached a high pass winding around to the other side of the mountain. This would do nicely, he thought—he didn't need to make it to the mountain's peak, he needed only a look at what lay on the other side.

He snugged his lionskin tighter around his shoulders. By the gods, it was getting cold. An icy wind swept down off the snow on the mountain's peak. He paused for a moment to rest, watching his breath plume in the air before him. Then, taking a deep breath, he started around to the other side of the mountain.

Something dark in the snow fifty feet above caught his

eye. It was half buried, but from the shape, he knew it couldn't be natural.

He hesitated, searching for an easy way up, but didn't find one. Shrugging, he scrambled up a steep, rocky slope. Then he came to ice and had to tread more carefully. His fingers grew numb from the cold, but he pulled himself higher until he came to that patch of darkness.

He found himself staring down at the head of a my-serae. Frozen in the snow, only its head and part of its right wing stuck out. Its skull had been half eaten away by rats or mice or carrion birds, but he couldn't mistake that long, cruelly sharp black beak.

King Muros had lied. The creatures did live here.

He hesitated, considering how to get the myserae out of the snow and ice, but finally he decided to leave it there. Jason would believe him without proof. And if King Muros planned some treachery, it would be best if he didn't suspect they knew of his lies.

Hercules slid down the snow, returning to the pass, then continued on. He hadn't come this far to turn back now.

As he rounded the mountain, he saw the dazzling blue-green curve of the shore far below, but here jagged black rocks and high, pounding waves made it inhospitable to ships; there were no towns or settlements of any kind, only wild forest. Quickly he scanned the sky, but he saw no sign of other myserae. They might well be back in Thorna, he reminded himself, terrorizing the villagers.

Shaking his head, he started back. His little trip had taken long enough; he needed to be there when Atalanta returned with the bearers. He couldn't let King Muros suspect anything.

From the *Argo*, Orestes watched the preparations for that night's feast with growing anticipation.

The king's servants set up red-and-white-striped pavilions on the beach two hundred yards away. Musicians came out and tuned their lyres. Acrobats smoothed the sand with long wooden rakes and took practice tumbles, or walked on their hands, or balanced on each others' shoulders. A feeling of high festivity rode the air.

Half the crew had gone ashore to help. He watched Hylas and Maenar and a dozen other Argonauts helping to set up tables and benches. Other Argonauts were helping to dig barbecue pits and pile wood inside them.

It would be quite a celebration, Orestes thought. Even so, he couldn't help but wonder if Jason's speculation might not be true . . . if these people might not be planning to attack them tonight. That's why he had carefully kept ten well-armed men aboard the *Argo*.

Biting his lip, he waited and watched and pondered everything and everyone around him.

By the time Hercules made it down the mountain, Atalanta had already left. She hadn't been gone long, though—the crows hadn't yet descended to feast on the bodies of the bears.

He sat with his back against a tree to keep watch, the two spears he'd left behind beside him. Birds chirped happily; small animals rustled in the underbrush. Everything remained calm and peaceful.

Not long after his arrival, he heard excited shouts and the sounds of breaking branches and trampling feet. He rose, and then Atalanta led a dozen bearers into the little clearing.

"There they are!" she said, pointing to the bears.

Muttering excitedly among themselves, the men set to work skinning and butchering the carcasses. As they did, Hercules drew Atalanta to one side and in a low voice told her what he had discovered.

She nodded, frowning. "Then it's as Jason suspects—a trap."

He had to agree.

*   *   *

The procession back to the city was a triumphant one. Everyone had found game—Muros and Jason had taken five deer between them, Theseus's party had routed a family of wild pigs, and the king's cousins had a brace of rabbits, pheasants, and other small animals. Everyone marveled that Hercules and Atalanta had killed two bears. The king seemed most excited by it.

"This will be a feast to remember!" Muros proclaimed for all to hear. "Never have I or any of my hunters killed two bears on a single hunt!"

"Hercules is one of the greatest hunters in all Greece," Atalanta agreed.

"And Atalanta's skill with a bow is unequaled," Hercules added, grinning.

In all the excitement, though, Hercules found himself unable to talk to Jason alone. He desperately wanted to tell the prince of the myserae he had discovered in the snow, but realized he would have to wait until they returned to the city.

Unfortunately, everything seemed to be happening with almost painful slowness. And when the hunting party started back for the city, Hercules again found himself in the same chariot with Atalanta. He could only watch Jason in the chariot ahead and wait impatiently for their next meeting alone.

It was mid afternoon when they rode through the city gates. Jason felt exhausted and knew he needed to rest to be ready for tonight. And by the anxious way that Atalanta and Hercules kept looking at him, he knew that they wanted to speak to him alone.

As servants bustled off with the meat from the hunt, stable boys and grooms hastened to take care of the horses. Other servants took their weapons and helped wash the dust of travel from their hands and faces.

"You must pardon me," King Muros told Jason, wiping his hands on a cloth, "while I check up on preparations for our celebration. Would you like to return to your rooms to freshen up?''

"Thank you, but I must get back to the *Argo* to check on my men," Jason said firmly. "I want everything to go smoothly tonight, and I won't be able to enjoy myself unless I know everything is well with my ship."

"Of course, of course," Muros murmured distractedly. "Then I will see you later, on the beach."

Jason bowed and turned to lead the way to the *Argo*. Several of Muros's guards made to fall in with them as escort, but he waved them away with an easy laugh.

"I'll be able to find my way in the daylight," he said.

"As you wish," their captain said with a frown. He did not look happy about leaving them on their own, but Jason didn't care.

As they started through the streets, he turned to Hercules and said, "What is it you want to tell me?"

Hercules licked his lips, then launched into a brief recounting of his trip up the mountain, concluding with his discovery of the body of a myserae frozen in the snow and ice.

"Interesting," Theseus said. "It confirms our suspicions. Muros lied."

"But he seemed so believable . . ." Hercules sighed. "You can't trust anyone these days."

"But *why* would he lie?" Jason demanded. "What could he possibly gain from protecting the myserae? Does he *want* them destroying other islands?"

"Perhaps he made some sort of unholy truce with the creatures," Atalanta said. "They do not seem to bother him or his people, after all . . ."

Jason remained grim. "We will find out tonight," he said firmly, "one way or another."

Soon, King Muros thought, *they will be mine.*

It was still an hour till dusk. He stood on his city's walls, looking down on the *Argo*. About half of Prince

Jason's crew stood on deck, watching the start of festivities. The rest had already joined the crowds on the beach. Some danced with local girls, linking arms in long chains; others toasted each other, growing drunk on the summer wine he had provided from his cellars.

"Highness," a voice said behind him.

He looked over his shoulder. It was Vargas, his chamberlain.

"What is it?" he said.

"Highness, my father has taken deathly ill. I wish to visit him in his last hours, if I may. Tertes is able to serve as your chamberlain tonight."

It was strange to think of Vargas as having a father—he seemed, somehow, eternal. But Muros felt festive, and it didn't really matter. Tertes, his chamberlain-in-training, could do the work as well as anyone.

"Very well," he said, "you have my permission. Take as long as you need, Vargas. Such matters are often delicate."

"Thank you, Highness. I expect to return tomorrow. I have been told my father will not live out the night." He bowed and shuffled away.

And now I must join the celebration, King Muros thought. His clothes were already set out: a fine gray tunic with silver doves embroidered around the sleeves. With it lay a small sword. He smiled as he picked it up and tested the sharp bronze blade with his thumb. *Yes. I might even kill Hercules myself,* he thought.

As darkness fell, Jason wandered through the crowds of feast-goers, nodding politely to the few nobles he recognized from the banquet the night before. Laughter echoed; musicians sang; dancers leaped and cavorted around the bonfires. It was, he thought, quite a celebration, and one he would have fully enjoyed in better circumstances.

He wore his finest blue tunic. It wasn't really cool

enough for a cloak, but he had donned one anyway; it concealed the small sword he wore.

"Jason!" a loud voice boomed as a heavy hand slapped him on the shoulder. Jason rolled his eyes toward Olympus. Hercules had been drinking heavily, becoming ever more boisterous as the celebration grew.

"You shouldn't drink so much," Jason said. "You want to be fresh for the battle, don't you?"

"Oh, I'm looking forward to it. Now this is the sort of life I like—excitement, fighting, and good wine!"

"Keep your voice down!" Jason turned. Hercules was dressed much like he had been the night before, in his lionskin, with only a small knife at his side. He had a small amphora of wine in one hand, and a trickle of wine ran down his chin.

Hercules laughed. "Have some!"

"Did you notice," Jason continued in a whisper, "that the king's guards aren't drinking anything but water? And that they outnumber us three to one? And that they're all in armor with their weapons at hand?"

"Sounds like a fair fight, eh?"

"Hercules . . ." Jason sighed. "Fights aren't supposed to be fair, they're supposed to be won. *Easily.* By us."

Hercules grinned. "How long before they attack?"

"I haven't seen our host yet. They will probably rush us when he arrives. He won't want to miss the excitement, after all."

"What about you? Didn't you bring a sword?"

"Beneath my cloak." He raised it enough for Hercules to glimpse the hilt. "And you?"

"Oh, I'll make do with whatever's at hand." He winked. "It's more fun that way. So . . . shall we start things ourselves, instead of waiting for the king?"

"No," Jason said. "Now that we know they're up to something, we should rally the—"

"That's no fun!" Hercules cried. A pair of the king's guards were passing. In one quick motion, Hercules leaped upon them, bashing their heads together. As they collapsed, Hercules drew both their swords.

"—men," Jason finished. Sighing, he drew his sword. Perhaps Hercules was right, he told himself. Sometimes direct action *was* the best way. At least Muros wouldn't have time to organize his attack.

Screaming a battle cry, Hercules leaped for the nearest guard. The man stumbled backward, caught by surprise. Hercules struck him in the side of the head with the hilt of one sword, and the man collapsed, unconscious before he hit the sand.

"Argonauts—to me!" Jason cried, raising his sword in the air. "Argonauts, rally here!"

A dozen battle cries went up. Jason saw his men draw their concealed knives and swords. Several caught up burning sticks and wielded them as clubs. Metal rang on metal.

Then two guardsmen closed with Jason. He retreated quickly before them, parrying their wild swings again and again. They were off balance, used to firm ground underfoot rather than sand, and Jason kept them constantly moving, constantly shifting.

Finally, panting, they slowed their advance. The one to the left fell a half step behind, and that left an opening. Jason reacted instantly, lunging forward and running the guard on the right clean through.

Jerking his blade free, he closed with the other, screaming a savage battle cry. The man back-pedaled frantically, then stumbled and fell, sword flying from his hand. Jason punched him in the face with the hilt of his sword and he collapsed.

Half a dozen Argonauts ringed him now. A few guardsmen rushed at them, but his people held their own. Across the beach, he spotted Theseus, Orestes, and Iacoros. Some of the king's guards attacked them from the side. The Argonauts fought back savagely, driving their attackers off, and soon reached him.

"Hold our position here," he said grimly. More of his men joined him. Fighting was concentrated in knots up and down the beach, he saw now. All the commoners had fled in terror, and most of the nobles had followed right on their heels. That left only the guardsmen and the Argonauts, facing off around a half-dozen bonfires.

Those who weren't yet engaged rallied to Jason. Quickly he formed them up into a battle line. The men he had left on the *Argo* began carrying out shields and spears, which were swiftly handed out.

He glanced at Hercules, a hundred yards away and in the thick of the fighting. Hercules danced among the king's guards, shouting and laughing like a madman as he pressed his attack. Suddenly his opponents began to throw down their weapons and run.

The Argonauts gave a loud cheer.

"It's not over yet!" Jason shouted. "Forward! Take the beach!"

His men began to march toward the city, beating their swords on their shields in a marching rhythm. More of the king's guards fled. Others tried to stand, and again it came down to hand-to-hand combat.

Jason lost track of the time. The battle became a blur of slashing, parrying, lunging. Blood roared in his ears. He felt his sword bite deep into flesh and bone again and again—

Until suddenly he looked up and found no one left to fight. All the guards had either died or fled. Most of his Argonauts held captured swords and helms, laughing and shouting of their victory. He could see only three of his crewmen lying dead or badly injured.

Muros's guards had been ill-trained for real war. From the number of bodies, Jason guessed that at least three-quarters of them had run away. He shook his head in disgust. Such lack of discipline would never have been tolerated in Thessaly or any of the other Greek states.

As he wandered across the battlefield counting the

dead, he noticed one of King Muros's advisors among them—Keros, whose throat had been messily cut. Jason distantly remembered the counselor trying to direct the battle at its beginning . . . but apparently the man had died before his strategies could be put to work.

Unfortunately, King Muros was not to be seen anywhere. That meant he hadn't made it to the beach before the fight began. Well, they would have to find him in his palace, then.

"To me, Argonauts!" Jason shouted. "On to the city!"

FIFTEEN

MUROS WAS HURRYING DOWN THE path to the beach when the first peasant passed him, going in the opposite direction at a dead run. The boy's face was as white as sun-bleached bone. Dozens of other people swarmed up the trail after him, pushing their king aside in panic to escape. And then Muros heard the sounds of fighting, the battle cries of his men, the clank of striking swords. The battle had started. Why hadn't they waited for his signal?

Drawing his sword, he cursed as he shoved through his subjects, hurrying, eager to watch his guards triumph over Jason and his Argonauts. More peasants pounded by him.

Then he came upon Huron struggling up the path behind the others, and that made him stop and frown. Both his counselors should have been supervising the slaughter. What was going on? Who was in charge?

Huron heaved to a stop before him, panting wildly. He

clutched his chest with both hands. "Flee, Your Highness!" he managed to gasp.

"What?" Muros demanded. "In the middle of my triumph? Have you gone mad?"

"There is no triumph, Highness! The Argonauts attacked *us*—it's an ambush, a trap! Flee, Highness, flee! Your men are being butchered!" And then Huron darted past him and continued up the path, gasping and wheezing all the way.

Muros stood there in shock. The Argonauts had attacked his guards? How could they have known about his trap? Who told them?

Keros? Surely not! He'd trusted his advisor all his life. *Then where is he?*

It doesn't matter now, he thought. *What's done is done. I'll gather my men inside my city, then we'll attack the ship. My men outnumber them ten to one.*

He turned and ran up the path after the others, calling orders, trying to restore calm. Only then would they be able to defend the city.

Jason stared up at the closed gates and frowned. Archers now guarded the walls of the city, dark shapes moving against a glittering backdrop of stars.

Jason stood well back, shadowed in a grove of trees. He had found the archers' range easily enough (fortunately, they all seemed to be bad shots), and now he stood well out of their reach. He watched and waited and thought. Although the walls were only half manned, he had no intention of losing more of his men to Muros.

"What now?" Hercules asked, from his left.

"We wait till dawn. They won't sleep this night."

"And then?"

"I . . . haven't decided yet."

A scant hour had passed since the battle on the beach, but King Muros had managed to marshal his men and barricade himself inside his city. It was the one intelligent thing he'd done so far, Jason thought.

The puzzle intrigued him. He wanted Muros dead, but didn't want to risk any crewmen to kill him. And what of the myserae? How did they fit into all of this?

Theseus joined them, then Orestes.

"We can keep them up all night while we rest," Theseus said. "If only we had a way to get inside . . ."

"I have an idea," Hercules said suddenly.

"What is it?" Jason asked.

"Witta led us here—maybe her magic can get us inside."

"It's too risky," Orestes said. "Good never comes from magic."

"Seldom, not never," Theseus said slowly. "Jason? What do you think?"

Jason hesitated. "I don't like magic much," he said, "but we aren't an army. We can't hold a siege with fifty men. If Muros picks us off one by one, we will soon be at his mercy. He outnumbers us badly."

"You wouldn't know it, the way his men fight," Hercules said.

"We took them by surprise. By day, they might overrun us."

"True . . ." Theseus said.

"I'll ask her," Jason said. "If there's anything she can do, I think it's worth a try."

He turned and raced down the winding path toward the ship. His thoughts flew ahead to the priestess and her magic. He knew little of her powers, but surely she could do something to get them past the gates and those archers.

By the time he reached the *Argo*, he had practically convinced himself of Witta's ability to rip the city from its foundations, to summon huge monsters from the depths of the sea, to raise armies of long-dead soldiers to fight their battle. Thoughts of destruction and revenge made him tremble with excitement. Swearing he'd see King

Muros dead before daybreak, he darted up the ship's gangplank, passed the two men he'd posted on sentry duty, then stopped in front of Witta's cabin. She was chanting softly within. He paused for a second, listening, then knocked.

Slowly, the hatch swung open. Darkness moved inside. He could see nothing ahead but shadows.

"Witta?" he called. No answer came. "Witta?"

He entered. The air felt thick and stifling. When he turned around and tried to look through the open hatch, he found nothing before him but velvety blackness. His eyes ached. He squeezed them shut for a minute, then groped his way forward.

Sudden, brilliant light flared. Blue-white afterimages blinded him. Softly a single finger, all a-tremble with age, touched the middle of his forehead, smearing what felt like oil or grease in a line down the bridge of his nose. Blinking rapidly, he found he could see again.

Witta stood before him. She was dressed all in black so that only her face showed, and it seemed to float loose in the air like a mask. And, still more like a mask, her eyes seemed empty hollows filled only with shadows and deep memories.

"Athena sent a dream," she said. "The myserae are here . . ."

"Yes!"

". . . and you must enter the city to stop them."

But she gave him no time to speak. Instead, she began to sing in a low, powerful voice, the words strange, unlike anything he had ever heard. Raising her hands, she made odd gestures in the air, her fingers shining like candles.

Jason found himself floating away from his body. Dizzy, he tried to steady himself. He looked down and saw his body far below, and a surge of terror swept through him. What had Witta done? Strange gray vapors swirled around his arms and legs and face. They seemed to pulse with an inner light. Distantly, as though in a dream, he felt his skin start to tingle. The mist covered him completely now. He began to struggle, but a strange heaviness weighted down his arms and legs.

"Witta—" he tried to say.

The vapors began to dissolve, revealing his body again. No, he realized, not his body, but that of a stranger . . . gray hair . . . long beard . . . wrinkles. Suddenly he realized he had become King Muros's elderly advisor, Keros. He opened his mouth; Keros opened his mouth. He blinked his eyes; Keros blinked his eyes.

He gasped . . . and was himself again. At once he raised his wrinkled, spotted old hands, staring at them in horror. Then he felt his long, pointed gray beard, the strange new lines of his cheeks and nose, and terror again welled up inside him.

"What have you done?" he cried.

"All who see you will see the king's counselor," she said. "All who hear you will hear his voice."

"But—"

"The magic," Witta said soothingly, "will not last for more than a few hours. When you will it, this appearance will fade and your former body will return. For now, use what Athena has given you to gain entrance to the city. I can do no more."

Jason shuddered. *I never should have come here. I never should have asked her for help. What if she made a mistake and the magic* doesn't *end? What if I look like Keros for the rest of my life?*

He backed from the room, out onto the deck, and when the sentries leaped forward with battle cries, he knew Witta's disguise to be perfect. *Too* perfect.

"It's me—Jason!" he called, raising his hands.

They drew up short, staring. At least he knew he needn't fear discovery, he thought with a sigh. Well, it was done: he would have to make the best of it. And if it could get them into the city . . .

"Jason?" Hylas asked softly. "How—"

"It's Witta's magic. There's no time for questions—remain on guard here. We will take the city tonight, with Athena's help!"

King Muros stood silently on the wall of his city, looking down on Jason's camp. The man mocked him, he thought, with his camp set up just outside the archers' reach.

He turned his gaze to the sea, to where the *Argo* sat tied up at his docks. He wanted that ship more than ever . . . almost as much as he wanted Jason dead.

He shivered, suddenly cold, and gathered his cloak tighter around his shoulders.

"Keep watch," he told the captain of his guard. When he turned to go back down, the man suddenly stiffened.

"Sir!" he said, pointing out toward Jason's camp.

"What is it?" Muros whirled, staring out into the darkness. An attack? No—a lone figure moved forward. A spy, or perhaps a messenger?

"Archers!" he called. Around him, men leaped to their places, stringing arrows.

A distant shout came to his ears: "Wait, Your Highness! It's me, Keros! Open the gate!" Muros could hear him panting.

Turning, Muros called for a torch. A guardsman carried one up from the courtyard, then tossed it over the wall, toward the figure below. It struck the ground and almost went out, but the man there picked it up and held it so the light shone in his face. It was indeed his counselor, Muros saw. Only, Keros had been reported dead on the beach. Perhaps he had merely been knocked unconscious; things like that happened in battle, or so the old stories said.

"Your Highness, let me in!" Keros called again.

"What trick is this?" Muros called down suspiciously. "Why would the Argonauts let you go?"

"I bear a message for you from Jason himself. He released me that I might bring it to you."

"Very well. Wait." Muros stepped back, stroking his chin in thought. It might be a trap . . . but he saw no unusual movement beyond the walls. The Argonauts had not massed for an attack yet. Perhaps they realized how badly outnumbered they were and wanted to negotiate. The least he could do was to listen to their terms.

"Let him in," he called down to the gatekeepers.

Ten minutes later, Muros met with his two counselors and his new captain of the guard in a private meeting room. He found his mood improving. Now that he had both his counselors back, now that they were within the city walls, he knew they were safe. From here, they could rally their troops, pick off Jason's men one at a time, and finally drive the Argonauts away . . . or take their ship once and for all.

"We must, of course, attack," Huron was saying to Keros and Eragon, the new captain of the guard. "Our troops outnumber theirs. It should be an easy battle."

"I disagree," Keros said. "They slaughtered our men on the beach, and there we outnumbered them ten to one!"

"We were taken by surprise."

"Half the men fled!" He turned to Eragon. "That's battle discipline?"

"Discipline will improve under me," Eragon said sharply. "I cannot be blamed for what happened on the beach. I wasn't in charge there!"

What would my father have done? Muros wondered. Everyone continued to argue around him. Finally he could take it no longer.

"Shut up, all of you!" he snapped. "I won't have you bickering like old women! *I* will make the decisions." He turned to Keros. "Now, you said you had a message from Jason?"

"He offers you terms of surrender which, I should imagine, you will reject out of hand."

"Tell me what they are."

"Simply this, Your Highness: open the gates, have the guards surrender, and let him and his men occupy the city. In return, they will leave as soon as they empty your treasury. 'The price of treachery,' I believe he called it. In further return, they won't kill anyone except you."

Muros was outraged. "Kill *me*?"

Eragon nodded. "That's very generous of him, all things considered, except for the last part."

"Well," Huron said, "I suppose you want to take their offer. Typical of the military mind!"

"Perhaps he's willing to negotiate the terms?" Eragon asked, with little hope.

Keros shook his head sadly. "He made himself quite clear. The terms are not negotiable. It's a matter of honor, the prince said. For betraying the laws of hospitality, he wants Your Highness dead."

While the others thought about that, Muros reached a decision. *After all,* he thought, *we can outlast their siege anyway. What difference does it make? None.*

He said: "We will stay right where we are. We have deep wells and plenty of stored provisions; we will wait them out, no matter how long it takes. Our archers can pick them off if they get too close."

"As you command, Highness," both his advisors said. Eragon merely saluted.

"Now get out and leave me alone! I need to think."

They bowed, turned, and filed through the door. As it shut behind them, Muros again wondered what his father would have done.

This is my chance, Jason realized.

He stood by the door leading into the front courtyard, listening to the silence outside. By the light of the torches flickering in the breeze, he saw the still, dark shapes of guards slouched on the battlements. They were sleepy; nothing short of a direct attack would rouse them now.

Drawing his knife, Jason tucked it into the sleeve of his tunic and smiled. Then he pushed the door open a bit more, wincing as the hinges squeaked, and eased out into the shadows.

Across from him stood the main entrance. The gate-keeper, a gnarled old man who looked almost as ancient as Witta, leaned on the giant wooden wheel he turned to open the enormous main gates. He snored softly.

The machine's counterweights, gears, and pulleys all lay out of sight somewhere belowground, Jason saw, but he didn't let that stop him. He'd seen mechanisms like this in Athens. They were childishly simple to operate.

He circled the courtyard as if making one last inspection before turning in for the night. The two bleary-eyed guards he passed saluted him. Smiling, he nodded back and murmured, "Keep up the good work."

He reached the gates unchallenged. Overhung by the battlements, they lay deep in shadow. In one quick glance, he noted the heavy oak bar across them, which way the wheel turned to open them, and what he needed to do.

Lifting the heavy bar carefully, he maneuvered it to the ground, trying not to grunt as his muscles strained and he nearly dropped it. Then, done, he approached the gate-keeper, drawing his knife. One quick blow across the temple and the old man slumped forward, unconscious.

Jason pushed him aside and began turning the wheel to the right. The gates shuddered, then started to move, at last gliding open on well-oiled leather hinges.

"Hey!" someone said behind him. "What do you think you're doing?"

Jason turned and waved. "King Muros's orders." The gates stood wide open now. "I'll take care of it."

The guard ran toward him, sword in hand.

A rope ran from the wheel and disappeared into a slot in the stone at Jason's feet. He knelt and sawed at it with his knife. The fibers parted easily. At last the final strand gave way and the rope whipped past him, down the hole and out of sight. He heard a distant *whump* from somewhere underfoot, as though a great weight had fallen.

The guard came to a stop before him, looking bewildered. "King Muros *ordered* you to—"

"Well, no," Jason said. "I lied." Then he threw the knife fast and underhand, and it struck the guard's neck. He fell with barely a gurgle, clawing at the blade.

Jason didn't wait. Scooping up the guard's sword, he raised it and gave a piercing whistle.

Another whistle answered from the darkness outside the city. The road to the main gate suddenly swarmed with life as forty men in battle gear charged forward. Each carried a round leather shield over his head as protection against arrows, and they all screamed their most fearsome war cries. At their front ran Hercules, brandishing a sword in one hand, holding his shield before him with his other.

"Take the walls first!" Jason shouted to them. They all knew his plan and recognized him as their commander, despite his disguise.

They poured through the city's gates just as the alarm went up among the guards on the battlements. A few arrows flew, but the defense was halfhearted at best, with the city gates standing open. Jason led the way up the steps to the top of the wall. His Argonauts had gained entrance to the city without suffering a single wound, he saw proudly.

Most of the archers threw down their bows and fled their positions the moment they saw the Argonauts approaching. Jason knew that, at this rate, it wouldn't take long to rout the entire city.

"What now?" Hercules demanded, drawing to a halt beside him. Others continued along the walls, making sure no archers remained.

"Split up," Jason said. He gestured to a group of about twenty. "Theseus, rush the guardhouse. Take prisoners if they surrender. Otherwise, show no mercy.''

"Yes, sir!" Theseus said. Turning, he ran for the stone stairs leading downward, a dozen men at his heels.

"What of us, Jason?" Hercules asked. He seemed remarkably restrained. "King Muros?"

"King Muros—and the palace!"

With a roar, Hercules waved to the rest of the men. "To victory!"

Everyone raised his sword and shield, echoing. "To victory!"

"And a double share of the loot to the man who finds King Muros and brings him back alive!" Jason added.

Another cheer went up among the Argonauts. Then they surged forward, splitting up into small groups. Atalanta headed one, Orestes another, and Orpheus a third. Only Hercules remained behind. As Jason watched, his people poured through the doors onto the main courtyard of the palace, and in seconds he heard the sounds of fighting from within, swords ringing, shouts, curses, and the screams of the dying and the wounded.

"Shall we join them?" Jason asked, drawing his own sword.

"Yes. I'll kill Muros myself!" Hercules vowed.

"Not if I find him first!"

They looked at each other, grinning madly.

"A contest?" Jason said. "Winner gets Muros all to himself?"

"Agreed!" Hercules cried. He turned and ran for the nearest door, getting a quick lead. But Jason moved as fast as a cat and sprinted after him.

The main doors stood open. Jason pounded into the audience chamber and hesitated for a second, looking around. Guttering torches along the walls provided dim light. Several bodies were sprawled on the floor, pools of blood forming around them, and one lay draped across King Muros's throne, princely in death. From the left, in one of the antechambers, Jason heard the sharp, ringing clash of sword on sword. Where would Muros be hiding? Slowly he turned, listening for any telltale sounds. To his right rose the huge stone staircase leading to the next floor.

Hercules returned from one of the side rooms. He had blood on his sword.

"Muros?" Jason called.

"Not here!" He started up the staircase, and without a moment's hesitation, Jason followed. Side by side they ascended at a breakneck pace, splitting up only when they reached the top and had to skirt a small battle. A pair of Muros's guards stood back-to-back, engaging a band of Argonauts, and they were managing to hold their own. Several of Hercules' people, including Atalanta, nursed bloodied arms where the two had scored.

"They're good," Atalanta told him. "Better than all the rest of Muros's men."

Ignoring the two, Hercules headed left, toward the far end of the hall and more sounds of swordplay. Jason paused for a moment to watch the fight. Atalanta had been right, he realized, and his surprise grew. These guards moved like a team, each covering for the other like only well-seasoned warriors could. Then Jason noticed the similarities between them: unlike Muros's people, each had strikingly blond hair beneath his helm, high cheekbones, a thin nose, and tightly set lips. For all their gauntness, they seemed surprisingly strong. Brothers? Mercenaries?

"Wait!" Jason called.

At once his men backed off. The two guards watched him warily, swords half-raised. The first wiped sweat from his eyes.

Jason looked them over, slowly circling. They shifted uneasily, like cats. Shock was apparent on their faces.

"Traitor!" one of them snarled.

"Traitor?" he said, puzzled. Then he remembered he still looked like Keros—Witta's magic had not yet worn off. He laughed and willed the illusion to end, concentrating as hard as he could. The air before him shimmered. When the heaviness on his face and body lifted, he knew the magic was gone. He stood before them as Prince Jason of Thessaly once more.

"Put down your weapons," he told them. "You won't be harmed; I give you my word. I see you're not of Muros's people, so I bear you no grudge. Where are you from?"

Cautiously, the one on the right shook his head. "To the far west, a land called Atlantis." He lowered his sword. "I am Réas. This is my brother, Emeras."

Jason nodded. "King Muros is doomed. This city will be ours within the hour . . . you can see what's happening. After this fight, we'll need more men for the *Argo*. If you're interested, I've got a place for both of you. What do you say?"

Réas hesitated. "Perhaps."

"Good." Jason nodded. "I assume you've been here long enough to learn your way around. Where is Muros's suite?"

Emeras pointed to the right. "That way. Turn at the corner, then you can't miss it. The doors are painted white and purple."

"Thanks." He started to the right, laughing to himself. *Hercules went the wrong way!* Then he turned back to Réas and Emeras, saying, "Find something else to wear. There'll be plenty of things in the nobles' rooms, so help yourselves. I won't ask you to fight the rest of the guards, just to stay out of the way for now. We'll get everything straightened out later."

Réas hesitated. "You seem a man of your word, but . . ."

"You don't know if you can trust me."

Both brothers nodded.

"I don't think you have much choice," Jason said, "but consider this: my every action here has been in response to King Muros's attempts to kill me and seize my ship. We meant him and his people no harm, and in fact, we are here to try to save the people of another village.''

''From the myserae.'' Réas nodded. ''I heard about your hunt for their island and your quest for the Golden Fleece. Is it true?''

''Yes.''

Réas hesitated for another second, then glanced at his brother, who nodded.

''Very well,'' Réas said. He sheathed his sword, as did Emeras. ''But we will not take up arms against our fellows. With your permission, we will withdraw from the city and await you on the beach.''

''Agreed,'' Jason said. He glanced to Atalanta. She should be able to keep track of them well enough, he thought. ''Will you escort them to a safe place?'' he asked.

She looked pained—after all, this would take her away from the battle, he realized—but she nodded. And it was just as well; her sword arm had a nasty looking cut that should be tended to quickly.

''Thank you.'' Turning, Jason continued down the hallway cautiously, then went around the corner and saw the white-and-purple doors just ahead. But, curse his luck, Hercules stood at the far end of the hall. Apparently he had come in a circle.

They both dashed forward and reached the doors at the same time. Hercules laughed.

''A tie!'' Jason said, grinning.

''Unless he isn't here.'' Hercules pushed at the door, but it had been barred from the inside and wouldn't open. ''All right,'' he admitted. ''We found him.''

''We'll rush it on the count of three,'' Jason said, stepping back.

Hercules followed, raising his sword.

''One . . . two . . . three!''

And on three, Hercules hurled himself at the door, just ahead of Jason. Its light wood shattered easily. He crashed through and sprawled onto the room's floor. With a sigh, Jason stepped over his friend's body, glancing around curiously.

It was a large, simply furnished room. Several low couches sat against the paneled walls. A large desk, covered with stacks of clay accounting tablets, stood in the center of the room. More tablets sat on the floor. Several low chairs seemed to have been hastily pulled aside.

Behind the desk, with swords drawn, stood Huron and Captain Eragon. They had probably sworn to defend Muros to the death, Jason thought, though they looked almost sick at the prospect. Behind them, also armed with a sword, stood King Muros himself. Muros's face was very, very pale. He swallowed visibly.

Jason took a fighter's stance as Hercules climbed to his feet and raised his sword.

Hercules was laughing. "I won!"

"By accident—you fell in!"

"He's still mine!"

"Oh, all right," Jason said. It didn't matter who killed Muros, as long as justice was done. "Take him, then. I didn't want to kill him that much, anyway."

They both took a step toward Muros. Then another.

To Heron and Eragon, Jason said, "I only want King Muros. If you both lay down your weapons, you won't be harmed."

"Huron, Eragon, you fools!" Muros cried. "You should have rushed them!"

Huron turned and glared at his master. "You have a sword. I didn't see *you* rushing them."

"Why, you insolent old—"

"Shut up, boy!" Huron snapped. "I'll run you through myself if you don't."

"No!" Hercules said, half jokingly. "Don't do that! He's mine!"

The three of them looked at Hercules, who slowly let his smile grow. He could be very intimidating in battle,

Jason realized, even without his reputation as the greatest hero of the age.

Jason advanced another step, making tiny circles with the tip of his sword, drawing their attention to his blade, while Hercules circled to the left.

Suddenly Hercules leaped forward, his sword a blur of motion as he attacked the captain of the guard. Eragon parried frantically again and again, and on Hercules' fourth blow, the captain's sword shattered like cheap pottery, making a dull, ringing sound. Hercules leaped forward, pressing his blade to the man's throat.

"Yield!" he demanded.

"My oath forbids it," Eragon said. He shoved Hercules back, then threw himself onto Hercules' weapon. There he hung for a moment, transfixed. Slowly he slid off. The bronze blade made a painful, metallic sound as it slid across bone.

"A good man," Hercules said solemnly. He looked up at Muros, a new fury in his eyes. "You did not deserve him."

Swallowing, Huron threw down his own sword, "Jason, I wish to surrender now!" He raised his hands.

"My, what loyalty you inspire, Muros," Jason said sarcastically.

Muros bit his lip. Then he lunged suddenly and ran his blade though his counselor's back.

A surprised look came over Huron's face. "Your Highness," he whispered. He winced as Muros wrenched the sword free, then he fell. Coughing, blood streaming from nose and mouth, he died with a low whimper.

Jason felt something tighten in his stomach and cursed softly. It was one thing to die in open battle. But to be stabbed in the back . . .

"For that," he told Muros in a cold, hard voice, "your death will be twice as long and twice as painful."

Holding his sword ready, Muros backed up to the wall. He kept glancing from Hercules to Jason and back again, the tip of his blade darting back and forth between them like some mad insect.

Then the wooden panel behind him slid open, revealing darkness. A gnarled hand reached out, seized Muros's shoulder and jerked him inside.

Jason gaped. King Muros yelped in surprise.

The panel slid shut with a click.

Sixteen

JASON STARED AT THE WALL, HARDLY daring to believe what he'd just seen. King Muros had been snatched out from under them.

Hercules ran forward and kicked the panel as hard as he could, but the wood didn't break. He struck it again and again, still with no effect, then backed up and stared at it.

"There must be a hidden catch," Jason said. He walked forward slowly, studying the wall, but didn't see anything unusual. The intricate woodwork could have hidden a hundred buttons, latches, or switches, though, and he never would have seen them. Theseus might have, considering how clever he was, but unfortunately, he had sent the Argonaut off to take the battlements.

Running his fingers over the panel, then over the molding around it, Jason found only dust and splinters.

He stepped away. "We'll need an ax."

"I'll find one," Hercules growled.

When Muros backed up to the wall, he thought he had only a few seconds left to live. Jason and Hercules moved closer, their swords ready. Then they both stopped and stared at something behind him, apparently surprised. But he knew that trick and didn't look. Instead, he tensed, preparing to fight. They wouldn't kill him easily, he vowed. If he took at least one of them with him, it would be enough.

Then a hand seized his shoulder from behind and pulled him into a secret passage he had never known existed. He yelped. The panel slid shut, locked with a click, and darkness surrounded him.

"Who's there?" he whispered. He found himself shaking all over. His hands trembled so much, he almost dropped his sword. "Your chamberlain, Highness," a familiar-sounding old voice said.

"Vargas?" He could sarcely believe it. "What—how—?"

Vargas spoke an odd-sounding word, and a dull reddish light flared all around them. Muros couldn't see where the glow came from. How was this possible? Could it be magic of some kind?

"Is that better, Highness?"

"Yes," Muros said. He shivered a bit, looking first one way, then the other. They stood in a cramped passage that smelled of dust and mold and ancient, rotting wood. The ceiling lay a scant hand's width over his head, and the walls were so close that two men could not have passed one another. How long had this secret passage existed? How could it be here without him having known about it?

"This way, Highness." Vargas turned and started to the left.

Muros caught his arm. "I asked you a question," he said insistently, setting his feet.

"If you want to live," his chamberlain said, "you will follow me now, without protest."

Muros hesitated. Jason and Hercules began banging on the secret panel. It sounded as though they might break through at any minute.

"Very well," he said. "Lead the way."

His chamberlain started forward again, and he followed, all the while marveling at the cunning way the passage twisted and turned. It divided a dozen different times, but the old man never hesitated; he seemed to know the route well, as though he had traveled it many times before. And the strange red glow continued to follow them, though Muros could not see where it came from.

But how could he know of it? Muros kept wondering. As a boy, he had grown up in this palace. He had explored every nook, every secret room and corridor. And yet he had never been here before.

The passage wound steadily downward, deeper and deeper into the earth. The floor turned to solid bedrock and sloped steeply; the walls became stone, which glistened with seeping water.

"Where are we going?" Muros demanded. Could they be heading toward the beach? He had lost all sense of direction and couldn't be sure. He *did* know that they were already far below the city. Vargas said nothing. He didn't even glance over his shoulder to make sure Muros was keeping up with him.

The king gave up asking questions, and they continued in silence for a time. Finally the tunnel widened and became a natural cave, with stalactites and stalagmites and all manner of strange rock flows draped like carpets around them. Staring all about him at the cave's unearthly beauty, Muros didn't notice that his chamberlain had stopped until he bumped into the old man.

Vargas rounded on him, glaring. "Be careful!"

Muros snapped, "How dare you speak to me that way! I—"

He broke off suddenly as a weird chirping sound echoed from ahead. He shivered, unnerved. What sort of beasts lived in caves like this? He imagined giant bats and slimy, winged things with bulging white eyes and razor-sharp claws. Then he thought of the underworld. Could they be in Hades?

Fingering his sword, he peered as far ahead as he could, but saw only darkness. Yet something seemed to be moving there . . . something *huge*.

Abruptly, Vargas clapped his hands. The red glow went out like a lamp's flame suddenly snuffed, leaving them in utter darkness.

The strange chirping came again, louder than before, nearer. Muros tensed, a thousand fears running through his mind. He heard the clicking noise of clawed feet—

And then he saw the glowing red eyes.

By the time Hercules returned with an ax, Jason had just about given up hope of ever catching King Muros in the secret passage. Five minutes had passed, more than enough time for anyone to escape. Muros could easily be in the wilds of Sattis by now, safe from reach. Or he might be sailing off to neighboring islands for help, or raising an army among the other towns and villages on the island . . . there *were* only fifty Argonauts, Jason reminded himself. They had won out thus far by courage, daring, and Witta's magical trickery. They would not have a chance against four or five hundred properly trained and equipped soldiers.

"Damn him," he whispered. Nevertheless, he moved back, giving Hercules room to swing the ax. Perhaps it was merely a secret room, he told himself. But no, if that were the case, they all would have hidden there, wouldn't they? Muros had looked downright shocked when someone pulled him inside.

Hercules raised the ax over his head, muscles rippling like water beneath his lionskin, and he tightened his grip on the haft. With a savage cry, he brought the ax down. It bit deep into the panel's wood. Wrenching it free, he struck again and again. Wood chips flew, and Jason moved back a few more feet when a splinter stung his cheek.

At last the panel shattered, and Hercules kicked it in the rest of the way. Grasping the ax in one huge hand, he started to duck through.

Jason grabbed his arm. "Wait," he said.

"He's mine!" Hercules roared. A battle fever had come over him, Jason realized. Right now he would follow Muros to the ends of the earth in search of vengeance.

He pulled his friend back. "Listen to me! He's gone, so forget about him for now. He has too much of a head start, and you don't even know which way he went, do you? Nor do you have a lantern. What happens if you get lost?"

Hercules took a deep breath, then shrugged a bit ruefully. "I hadn't thought of that."

"I'll tell you what happens," Jason said. "You wander around some more and maybe fall into a trap, or an ambush, or maybe you never find your way out again. Who knows how far that passage goes, or where? Muros and his men might well be waiting in ambush for *us*. Someone saved him, after all."

"So how do we catch him, then?"

Jason smiled. "For now, we don't. Have you forgotten the real reason we came? We have to find the myserae and stop them from destroying Thorna."

Slowly, Hercules nodded. "We still have a palace to capture. Come on!" Hefting his ax, he started for the door.

Muros stared at the eyes coming toward him. They were red and feral and seemed to burn like embers in the darkness. He caught a strange, sharp smell almost like an animal's musk, but unpleasant and unhealthy. He took several steps back.

Then an odd half-humming, half-crooning sound began. It raised the hackles on his neck and made him shiver uncontrollably. He realized suddenly that the sound came not from the creature—whatever it was—but from his chamberlain. The thought disturbed him. What was the old man doing?

A second voice joined the first—a harsher sound, full of chirps and squeals that no human throat could ever produce.

"Vargas?" he whispered. "What's going on? What are you doing?"

He took a step forward hesitantly. Before he knew what was happening, something hard struck him on the side of the head and he saw no more.

SEVENTEEN

B Y DAWN, HERCULES KNEW THE CITY was theirs. Everywhere he went, he found weapons lying underfoot—on the grounds or on the floors—cast down by guards who had fled their posts in terror. He grinned. Fifty Argonauts had taken a city of ten thousand—a deed fit for song! Then his expression soured. *If only we had captured King Muros, our victory would be complete.*

He came upon Atalanta and Theseus in an out-of-the-way corner of one of the courtyards. Atalanta had been wounded, though the injury did not look serious; Theseus was just putting away a bone needle and thread that he had used to sew up a sword cut on her right forearm. A couple of strangers in the uniform of Muros's guards stood behind them looking on curiously.

"Are you all right?" he asked Atalanta, eyeing the guards. They didn't seem to be prisoners.

"Well enough," Atalanta said, slowly flexing the fingers of her right hand. She winced. "I met my match in these two." She indicated the men behind her. "Jason was so impressed, he asked them to join our company."

Hercules raised his eyebrows a little. "High praise indeed," he said. He hoped they lived up to it. He knew the Argonauts must have lost a few good men this day, plus Nalos and Maenar, who had died fighting the cyclops on Thorna, so a few new swords would be doubly welcome.

"I'm Réas, and this is my brother, Emeras," the guard on the right said, inclining his head slightly.

He gave them a nod. "Hercules."

"We've heard of you," Emeras said.

"You know that Muros escaped?" Hercules went on to Atalanta and Theseus.

"Jason told us," Theseus said.

"I've spent the last few hours searching, but I haven't found a trace of him in the city. If he's here, he's well hidden."

"He would not stay," Emeras said. "His people . . . well, they do not love him as they loved his father. Someone would turn him in. Jason promised a huge reward for his head . . ."

Hercules nodded. "That's why I plan to ride up the coast and see if he came out on the beach. He may plan on hiding there until we leave. Care to join me?" He looked at Theseus. He really wanted someone to cover his back, and with Atalanta wounded . . .

"Gladly," Atalanta said, rising.

"Are you up to it?" Hercules asked her.

"Try to stop me!"

She seemed determined, so he nodded; he knew she would only be offended if he told her to stay behind. But he still wanted a strong, uninjured swordsman.

"And you?" he asked Theseus.

"I'm getting too old for these all-night battles," Theseus said with a laugh. "The only thing I crave right now is a bed!"

"Ah," Hercules said, a little disappointed. Then he looked to Réas and Emeras. They had not yet proven themselves to him in battle . . . but perhaps this would be the time for it.

Réas shook his head, though. "We will not fight our former master. Our oaths forbid it."

Hercules' respect for them increased. "I understand." He looked to Atalanta. "So it's just we two again. Let's see if there are horses left in the stables."

She rose smoothly. "A chariot?"

"Yes!"

Half an hour later they were racing down the beach in King Muros's personal chariot, pulled by a team of four spirited white horses. Dawn had long since fingered the east with pinks and golds, and now the sun shone down from a dazzlingly cloudless blue sky.

The sea to their left, a glittering blue-green near shore that deepened to azure farther out, was calm today. Low waves rolled in, and far out, dolphins leaped and splashed.

Hercules kept his attention focused on the rough land to their left for any sign of King Muros while Atalanta kept watch on the beach for tracks. They had passed a few outlying villages, then a scattering of farms and orchards, and had reached a wilder, untamed part of the island. Here the mountains came down close to the shore; jagged rocks and outcroppings could have hidden whole armies. Overhead, gulls wheeled and cawed, angry at being disturbed, so Hercules felt reasonably certain that no one waited in ambush.

Suddenly Atalanta gave a triumphant shout. "I see tracks!"

Hercules reined in the team of horses, and snorting and stamping, the beasts slowed. Sure enough—just ahead, two sets of tracks led down from the mountain and onto the beach. The trail led back into rocky foothills . . . to a small, almost hidden cave halfway up.

"That must be where the secret passage comes out," Hercules said, pointing.

Atalanta hopped to the ground and bent to study the tracks more closely. "But who—or *what*—is with Muros?"

Hercules dropped down and joined her. The tracks had to be several hours old and sand had crumbled into them, but he could see what she meant: two distinct sets of tracks came down to the beach. The first set, long and narrow, clearly belonged to a man. The second set, though . . . He squinted at it, imagining what sort of creature would leave a series of four deep indentations, three front claws, plus a large, heavy back claw.

"A myserae?" he whispered.

Atalanta bit her lip. "Why would it walk instead of fly?" she asked.

Hercules didn't have an answer for that. He stood, following the trail with his eyes. It led straight to the softly lapping waves along the beach, where it vanished. Clearly, they had gone to the firm, wet sand for better traction, and the incoming tide had obliterated any further traces of their passage.

"What now?" Atalanta asked.

Hercules hesitated. He wanted to follow Muros before the trail got any colder. But at the same time, something warned him that he'd need more men. *A myserae.* King Muros still had a few tricks, it seemed.

"Back to the city," he finally said, heading for the chariot. "Jason will know what to do."

By dawn, the city had completely fallen to the Argonauts. The commoners had locked themselves in their houses. The guards—those still alive, anyway—had either thrown down their weapons and fled, or surrendered peacefully, or been captured. And the nobles had all been rounded up and brought to the largest courtyard in the palace. They had offered no resistance.

Atop the palace walls, Jason looked down on them and sighed. What should he do with them now? They had the doomed, hangdog look of those who expected death at any moment. Their silence was oppressive and unnatural. The ladies looked particularly disheveled, with their fancy coifs in disarray, their elegant nightgowns ripped and soiled.

Jason sighed again and gazed out to sea. He had shown more mercy than any other conqueror would have done. His uncle would have razed the city to the ground, executed every guard and nobleman, and left Sattis a ruin. A part of him burned with that same rage, but he controlled and restrained it.

He and his Argonauts were *not* an invading army, he told himself. They were heroes on a quest. Their quarrel lay with King Muros alone, not with his people.

But first he had to deal with the people in the courtyard. Wearily, he turned to look them over once more.

Clearing his throat, he spoke to the guards: "We have no desire to see any of you dead. Our grudge lies with King Muros alone. For some reason, he tried to seize my ship and murder me. I have never done him any harm, nor did I intend to. Now a problem remains. What should we do with *you*? By all rights, you should be put to death, but I have no great desire for more bloodshed. Instead, you will be asked to put down your arms and swear not to take them up again so long as my men and I remain here. Those who refuse will be sent to live and work with the peasants outside the city walls—without weapons, of course. Those who obey may remain here, but confined to quarters."

An appreciative murmur went up among the soldiers and guardsmen. They seemed to like that idea.

Jason looked at the rest of his prisoners. "You nobles . . . ah, that's a different matter." He smiled at one of the ladies, who blushed and looked away. "You will be allowed to live within the palace as you always have. I will select a regent from among your number."

"We already have a king," one man called out. He held his head high despite his bonds and actually managed a kind of quiet dignity. "What of him? You cannot cast him out!"

"He will be killed," Jason said. "I have no doubt that he will try to recapture his city."

"But why can't you just take what you want and go? We can do you no harm now, nor can King Muros!"

Jason sighed. "I cannot leave Muros here alive and in power. It is a point of honor. We meant him no harm, and we would have left Sattis with good feelings and friendship between us. But his hospitality was betrayal. As his guests, we should have been under his protection. Thieves and assassins are not unusual in the world, but to have one in a position of power, ruling a land, is insufferable. These are crimes against custom and honor that can not be left to pass."

"I believe none of your fancy speech!" the man said. "You want to kill him!"

Jason smiled without humor. "As I just said."

"Then are you any better than King Muros?"

"The battle's over and my men hold the walls. If I were King Muros, you'd be dead by now. What do you think?"

The man snorted. He sat down again and stared at the paving stones.

Jason turned away, suddenly too tired to continue. "Theseus will see to all the details of your release," he said.

His old friend stepped forward and began calling orders, getting everyone on their feet and queued up. All at once the prisoners began to talk among themselves, and the babble of relieved voices rose to a deafening level. Jason winced, trying to shut out the noise. He decided, then and there, to return to his ship. On the *Argo*, at least he could rest for as long as he wanted without being disturbed.

He headed for the steps leading down to the courtyard. The excitement of battle had kept him going far longer than normally possible. Now his head throbbed and all he wanted to do was to crawl into bed and sleep for a good long while.

As he reached the courtyard, he saw Hercules and Atalanta run through the main gates. Hercules grinned and gave him a triumphant wave. Something had happened, Jason realized—good news? It had to be.

Hercules hurried over. He looked as fresh and well rested as ever, but Atalanta looked as bad as Jason felt. Jason forced a smile.

"What is it?" he asked.

"We found the king's trail!"

"How? Where?" He found himself breathing faster, his own excitement growing. If they could catch him—

"On the beach," Hercules said. "About a half mile from here, Atalanta spotted tracks leading from a cave. I think he's heading for the other side of the island. If we hurry, we'll catch him before nightfall!"

"How many are with him?"

"Maybe one. Maybe none." Hercules grinned. "There's an animal of some kind. I didn't recognize its tracks, but it's large enough that someone might be riding it."

"Are you sure it wasn't a horse?"

Atalanta said, "We know what a horse's tracks look like, Jason, even in sand. We thought—" She hesitated.

"What?"

"We thought they might be the tracks of a myserae."

"Walking instead of flying?" He frowned. It didn't seem very likely.

"It had claws," Hercules said, "just like the myserae. And it walked on two legs, like a bird. What else could it be?"

"I don't know. Nor does it matter."

"No," Hercules said. "Wherever he goes, we'll find him."

"And then," Atalanta said, "we'll kill him."

Muros woke to pain. It seemed to radiate from the back of his skull—wave after wave of excruciating, nauseating pain, as if his head had been staved in with a club. He risked opening one eye. The world blurred and swayed dangerously. Groaning, he closed the eye and wished he were dead.

"You're awake," a familiar-sounding voice said. "Get off. I'm tired of walking."

He opened both eyes this time. It took a tremendous effort, but the world stopped moving. His mouth was dry; he licked his parched, cracked lips with a tongue that felt like wool. Craning his head, he could just see Vargas standing beside him, looking dusty and tired.

Morning had come and they had made it to the beach, he saw. The sea lapped gently at the shore behind his chamberlain, sending pale blue fingers of water running up the sand.

Muros rubbed his eyes, straightened, stretched. Then he looked down and saw that he'd been lashed onto some sort of giant . . . black . . . *bat*?

He jerked upright and would have fallen off if not for the ropes around his feet. The creature beneath him waited calmly. It stood taller than a horse, and its leathery body bristled with tufts of coarse black hair. It wasn't a bat so much as an ugly, featherless bird, Muros realized. He rode high on its back, just behind the head. An oddly shaped leather saddle had been cinched around its chest and around its wing joints.

A jolt of fear ran through him. He began to struggle to get off, to get the ropes from his feet, to get away from the thing. His hands fumbled as he worked at the knots.

"It's a myserae," Vargas said in a soft voice.

Muros gaped. A myserae—those were the creatures Jason had come looking for! How had one gotten to his island? Why had he never seen one before?

"Pretty, isn't it?" Vargas continued. "I call this one Iolago. Its kind is older than humanity. Once, when the Titans ruled, they filled the skies by the tens of thousands, but now . . ." He shrugged. "Perhaps there are five hundred in the last colony. Still, that is more than enough for my purposes."

Muros stopped struggling and stared at him. "What purposes are those?" he asked sharply.

"I serve Hera. The myserae are sacred to her. I tend them, as my father tended them, and his father before him."

"Hera . . ." He had never thought the gods paid any attention to his island.

"You need help to regain your kingdom," Vargas said. "I have friends. This myserae is one of them. There are more like it in the mountains, and they will aid us, if I ask."

"I don't understand," Muros whispered.

"You don't have to. Trust me, Highness. Do as I instruct and all the Argonauts will soon be dead. And then you will rule Sattis again." He stepped forward and began to work at the ropes binding Muros to the saddle. "I have walked since before dawn. Change places with me now."

"Can it fly?" Muros asked, looking at the creature with new interest. If the myserae fought as well as Jason claimed they did, they might indeed make formidable steeds for an army.

"Of course. But I have only one with me, not two, and I would not abandon you here . . . and you could not control it properly if you tried to fly it by yourself."

He finished untying Muros's legs and stepped back. The king slid to the ground. Bending its neck, the myserae looked at him for the first time, and a wave of revulsion swept through him. It had two slitted red eyes (the ones he'd seen in the cave?), and it chirped softly to itself, then made a harsh coughing sound deep in its throat, a crow-like *caw*. The thing was *unclean*, he thought with a small shudder. It should be killed . . . killed and then its body burned to ashes.

Vargas clutched a small silver pendant hanging around his neck as he chirped back to the myserae and softly stroked its head. The pendant had been intricately worked to show a circle of myserae flying around the goddess Hera, Muros saw.

Swinging up onto the creature's back, his chamberlain made a gentle crooning sound. The myserae started forward at once. It waddled from side to side almost comically, but Muros found little cause for amusement. With its long legs, it moved faster than a man could walk.

Muros trailed slowly. What should he think? The Argonauts attacking, his chamberlain saving him, waking up on the myserae—it was all happening so quickly!

He knew he *had* to go with Vargas and the creature. He didn't have a choice right now. And if his chamberlain really could help him win his lands back . . .

He swallowed, knowing he would try anything, even an alliance with the myserae, to regain his throne.

EIGHTEEN

JASON PULLED ON THE REINS, SLOWING
the four black stallions pulling his
chariot. Miles of desolate beach
stretched out before him, broken here and there by outcroppings of black rock. Nothing moved ahead of him but
birds. The sun cast the waves in gold and silver, and a
magnificent sunset purpled the west. Behind him he heard
the clatter of wooden wheels and the creak of leather tack.
A horse whinnied.

He turned around and drove back to where Hercules
and Atalanta waited in their chariot, alongside Orestes and
Orpheus in theirs. The five of them had followed Muros
for mile after mile, losing his trail often as it got close to
the sea, then finding it again later. They had pushed their
teams of horses as hard as they dared, but Muros kept up
a steady pace (on foot, no less!) that they could not begin
to match. And, to Jason's bewilderment, he really did
seem to be accompanied by a myserae.

"Or the myserae is chasing him," Orestes speculated at one point.

Hercules had shaken his head at that. "It would fly after him," he said. "This one is walking alongside." Jason had to agree that it looked that way.

As the day wore on, the trail became older and older; Muros showed no sign of slowing for any reason. Finally Jason had called a halt. He drove half a mile ahead, saw that the trail continued up the beach without stop, and then drove back, shaking his head.

"Well?" Hercules called.

Jason said, "He isn't stopping."

"Then we'll have to ride faster!"

"No," Jason said, "we have to go back to the city."

"Why?" Hercules demanded. "We can still catch him, even if it takes all night!" Atalanta and the others echoed his words.

Jason sighed. Part of him—a large part—agreed with their feelings. Unfortunately, it just didn't make sense.

"He's moving faster than our horses are," he pointed out. "Now he's so far ahead that it could take days, or even weeks, to find him, and we don't have that much time. Remember, we're on a quest."

"We'll find the time!"

Jason shook his head. "Have you forgotten the myserae? They are our true reason for coming here. We can't spend all our time and energy chasing one man, no matter how much we want to."

"He's with a myserae . . ."

"One solitary creature. We need to find their nests."

Hercules chewed his lip, then nodded slowly. "You're right, of course. We must make sure the myserae are killed first. And then—"

"*If* there's time," Jason interrupted.

"—we can find Muros." Hercules turned his team of horses, heading back the way they'd come.

Jason sighed and rubbed his forehead. It was hot and

he was tired; the excitement of the chase had worn off hours ago. He hadn't slept in nearly two days now. Nevertheless, he found the decision painful. He'd been looking forward to punishing King Muros for his treachery.

King Muros trailed after Vargas and the myserae for hours. Most of the time he had to jog to keep up. His legs ached, and his chest constricted so he could hardly breathe. Much to his embarrassment, he had to beg his chamberlain to slow down several times. Reluctantly, it seemed, Vargas would oblige for a time—and then he'd continue as quickly as before, leaving Muros to stumble and follow as best he could.

As day faded into dusk, the land around them began to change. The beach grew rocky. Tall chalk cliffs rose to their right, and strange birds with bright feathers and hoarse, whispery cries circled high overhead. The sun— now the thinnest of crescents—touched the sea with its last rays and set the waves running with jags of gold and silver.

Still, Muros stumbled on. When he looked up, he saw Vargas ranging far ahead. He cursed under his breath, feeling his parched lips crack, and forced himself to greater speed.

Suddenly a stitch in his side made him wince. Tripping, he caught his foot between two stones and fell, twisting his ankle and skinning both hands and knees. He cried out in agony as a sharp, fiery pain shot through the length of his left leg.

Carefully he worked his foot free. For a long time he just sat there and nursed his ankle, no longer looking up, no longer caring whether Vargas abandoned him or not. He felt utterly beaten by the world. Shuddering, he closed his eyes and let his thoughts slip away. He just wanted to be safe.

Hearing the sharp clatter of feet on stones, he looked up and found Vargas glaring down at him from his myserae. The creature's eyes glowed faintly red in the twilight, lending it an ominous look. And, in the near dark, the chamberlain also seemed transformed. His face had taken on a hardness that seemed almost unnatural in someone so old. He held his body erect with a stiff-backed military bearing that spoke of both physical strength and inner confidence. In a strange moment of fancy, Muros thought the years were rolling back and that as he watched, Vargas was becoming younger. Then he realized their roles had somehow become reversed, with Vargas now master and he some disobedient underling.

"Get up," Vargas said. He clutched the pendant around his neck.

"I—"

"*Do it!*"

Muros found himself scrambling to his feet almost before he could think. The chamberlain's voice held a ring of command that somehow couldn't be disobeyed.

"Now follow me."

Vargas wheeled his myserae around. It hopped forward, talons clicking on small beach stones, a shadow moving into deeper shadows. Muros could barely see the glow of its red eyes. Cursing, trying to ignore the sharp pains in his ankle, he hobbled after them.

The world seemed to blur. Time stretched endlessly. The soft lap-lapping of the sea became a deafening roar that forced him onward, ever onward. At last he stumbled one final step and found himself a handbreadth from the myserae. He drew up, gasping. The creature had stopped. He could rest.

Vargas twisted around. The old man's eyes reflected the stars and the sea, cold and inhuman.

"Come," he said, almost gently. "Soon we will be there, my good king. We must leave the beach now."

Groaning, Muros forced himself upright. He couldn't feel his left foot anymore. A numbness had settled in: he didn't think, he just moved as commanded.

He followed the myserae up a break in the cliffs, up a wide ravine that had a few steps carved here and there to make the passage easier. Over his rough panting breath and the pounding of his heart, he heard Vargas chirping to his mount. He paused and leaned against the rock wall for a second, listening for the songs of night birds or the happy, familiar *chirrup* sounds of crickets in the scraggly grass. There weren't any. The silence was strange and unnatural.

Then Vargas called him and he found himself moving again, scrambling over rocks, heading steadily upward. He had to force himself to move one more foot, then another, then another.

At last, high up the mountain, they reached a wide ledge. A cave opened onto it. Somehow, Muros had the impression that this opening stretched deep into the heart of the earth. Far down its length he saw a faint glimmer of light. Torches? Did that mean people? He felt his heart starting to beat faster with anticipation.

Vargas paused for a moment, touching the pendant around his neck, and murmured something so softly Muros couldn't hear the words. The myserae waddled forward. Swallowing hard, Muros stumbled along behind them.

After fifty yards and several twists, the tunnel opened up into a vast, brightly lit cavern. It seemed all crystal and light, with huge gleaming spires and glittering facets. Muros gaped, stunned at the beauty of the place. It shone like a forest of diamonds. With every step he took, the pattern of light and shadow changed, and the walls seemed to dance around him. He saw himself reflected in the crystals' silver faces, his image multiplied and distorted until it became finally an unrecognizable blur.

Gradually he become aware of the myserae. They flew around and above him like phantoms in the night, soaring among the crystals with the grace of dancers. Slowly they landed, gathering around Vargas in the center of the cavern. The chamberlain chirped to them and they chirped back. The crystals seemed to catch the sound and carry it everywhere, turning it into an endless rhythmic burr.

Muros covered his ears to shut it out and pressed his eyes closed. This couldn't be happening, he kept thinking.

After a time, silence washed over him like an in-rushing tide. Slowly he peeked out and found himself surrounded by myserae. Their red eyes gleamed. Several cocked their heads to the side, staring.

They chirped several times, and two of them hopped back, leaving him room to move forward.

When he took a step, the myserae behind him inched forward. He stopped. Slowly they pressed up behind him, their leathery hides growing uncomfortably near. He took another step, suddenly nervous.

"Vargas!"

The echoes from his call brought no answer, no whisper of another human voice. His chamberlain had vanished.

What to do now? Wait for Vargas? Try to find him?

The myserae didn't give him a choice. They pressed closer, forcing him toward the rear of the cavern, crowding so that he had no place to move except onward. They seemed experienced with herding humans, he realized uneasily, as if they had done it before.

"All right!" he snapped suddenly, giving in. He limped forward, letting the creatures guide him. What else could he do? He wasn't in any condition to fight . . . not this many of them, anyway. He would need an army.

The far end of the cavern narrowed into a tunnel. The stone walls stood far enough apart that a half-dozen men could have marched through it side by side, but only two of the myserae could fit. The roof arched perhaps ten feet overhead. It, like the walls, had been carved from solid rock; in places, he saw chisel marks.

As he hesitated, they pressed up behind him again, wings just brushing the back of his neck, beaks opening and shutting with little snaps. He jumped forward, skin crawling. He felt a nagging sense of uncleanliness, as though they had left some sort of filthy residue on him. He resisted the impulse to try to brush whatever it was away. He wouldn't show any weakness. He swore it over and over to himself.

Still they forced him on, and finally the tunnel opened onto a large circular room with dozens of tall, glowing crystals embedded in the walls at regular intervals. They provided enough light to see with. In the center of the room, the stone floor had been marked off with a series of concentric rings, the first decorations Muros had seen since entering the underground, and in the center of the rings stood the statue of a goddess . . . Hera!

Muros gaped at the figure of the Queen of the Gods. Her beautiful but cruel stone face gazed down at the myserae as if blessing them. Her hands were outstretched in apparent welcome.

Muros shivered, more terrified now than ever before. *The myserae are Hera's creatures,* he thought, and then he remembered the silver medallion Vargas wore, the one with Hera's face on it. Could he be a priest of hers? Someone who guarded the myserae? Someone who kept his people safe from them?

The myserae did not give him time to think. Again they crowded him forward, into a small room perhaps ten feet square. Water slowly dripped from the ceiling, spattering into a shallow stone basin that jutted from one wall, while the overflow trickled down to a small hole in the floor. A straw pallet lay on the floor. It stank of mildew.

The place resembled nothing so much as a dungeon cell, he thought, but without the bars. He glanced back. Two of the myserae settled down outside his cell. Guards? They had to be.

Muros picked the driest spot and sat down with his back to the wall, ignoring the smell, ignoring the myserae. He could have wept. But something inside him hardened at the thought of Jason and Hercules and all the Argonauts looting his city, and he began to dream of vengeance.

NINETEEN

"THIS IS A MAP OF THE ENTIRE IS-
land," Theseus said, spreading out
the tightly rolled parchment before
Jason. "I found it in the palace library."

After his return from trying to track down Muros, Jason
had collapsed and slept straight through until noon. He
had awakened feeling refreshed. Theseus had been waiting for him with the map.

As Jason leaned forward, studying the spine of mountains running down the center of the island, he pointed
twice. "This is where Hercules found the dead myserae,"
he said, indicating the spot just inland from the city, "and
here is where we lost the king's trail." He frowned as he
studied the hills and mountains on the map. There were
no settlements on the south side of the island, but as he
recalled the rocky hills that bordered the sharp, inhospitable mountains there, he knew why. The map confirmed
his impression: the north side had open land and several

small rivers, perfect for farms and orchards.

"The myserae must live far from the civilized part of Sattis," Theseus said. "I have questioned dozens of people about them. One old fishermen claims to have seen giant birds far away in the sky, but he is the only one."

Jason studied the map again. "There seems to be a natural harbor here, just ahead of where we gave up on Muros's trail. That might be a good spot to begin our search for the myserae."

"When do we go?" Theseus rolled up the map and tucked it away. "Hercules led another expedition to the valley while you were sleeping. They should be back before long, but they will be tired."

"Tomorrow is soon enough," Jason said. "How goes the ship?"

"Repairs from the storm damage are complete. The hull has been recaulked and is as good as new. We have also restocked all our provisions—the palace's stores were abundant—and our water supply is fresh."

"And the palace treasury?"

"Safely aboard." Theseus grinned. "Several hundred gold and silver ingots confiscated from the royal treasury, plus our host's personal jewelry collection—dozens of rings, plus crowns, broaches, pins and pendants, and various jewels of dubious quality. And several pieces of ivory. Every time we find another cache of something worthwhile, we add it to the hold."

"Whether we find the Golden Fleece or not," Jason said, nodding, "we'll all return wealthy from this expedition."

Hearing a loud chirping, Muros leaped to his feet and faced the entrance to his cell. Dark shapes moved outside. Had the myserae come for him? What did they want?

He tested his injured ankle, slowly putting his full weight on it. It seemed much better; the swelling had gone down and he felt only a dull, distant ache when he stood normally.

"I trust you rested well, Highness," a familiar voice said from outside.

"Vargas!" Muros cried with relief. "Where have you been?"

Vargas wore a tunic as white as new milk. The silver pendant still hung around his neck, his only adornment. With his long white hair neatly combed, with his hands neatly manicured, Muros thought he looked ready for some high festival. Only the pinched, hard expression on Vargas's face spoke of the seriousness of the situation.

"On your business, of course, Highness."

"I didn't know what to expect, after the way you abandoned me here."

"Abandoned, Highness? Surely not . . . you were left among friends."

Muros shuddered. With friends like these, he scarcely needed enemies. Then he remembered the statue of Hera and asked Vargas about it.

"It was she who saved the myserae when Zeus and his brothers wrested control of the earth from the Titans," the chamberlain said softly. "She brought them here, gave them this home, and protected them. Now they serve her, just as I serve her. I am her eyes and her ears on Sattis. I nurture and protect the myserae, for they will serve her loyally all the rest of their days."

"I thought you served *me*."

"I serve the greater good of all on Sattis . . . you, the myserae, and Hera."

"But what of the myserae? I remember Jason's tale of what they did to Thorna. What of *my* people?"

Vargas shook his head. "The myserae are friends. They are going to help you reclaim your island. They would never hurt you, at least," he added ominously, "not while *I* am here."

"Then why did they keep me a prisoner?" He indicated

the stone chamber behind him. "I keep condemned men in better cells than this!"

"It was merely for your own protection." Vargas made reassuring motions with his hands. "You needed time to rest and recover from your escape. But come now, our plans have been made. The myserae are massing. All they need is you . . . for you shall lead them to victory!"

The tunnel sloped sharply upward, then wound to the left. As Muros walked, he pondered Vargas's words. Plans . . . myserae . . . a coming battle. Could he do it? Could he lead them in battle against Jason and the Argonauts?

Could he *not* do it? How could he possibly let Jason take the island that rightfully belonged to him? What would his father have thought? He blushed. No. He had to win back control of Sattis at any cost.

Ahead he could see brilliant light spilling into the tunnel; the crystal cavern lay just around the next turn. He had to talk to Vargas now, he knew, for he'd never get a chance before the fight.

He stopped and turned. "Vargas?"

His chamberlain sighed wearily. "Yes?"

"It's all happening so fast! What if we're making a mistake? What if—"

His chamberlain looked thoroughly disgusted. "You'd abandon Sattis to those foreign butchers?"

"No, never! But what if they've sailed on? What if we show up and there's no one there to fight? What then?"

"They are still in Sattis."

"How do you know?"

"I have seen them."

"But—"

Vargas tried to push him forward, but Muros grabbed the old man's arm and swung him back.

"You forget your place!" Muros said sharply. He wasn't used to people treating him this way, and he wasn't going to put up with it, not from a chamberlain, not from anybody.

Vargas's face reddened. His right hand moved toward the pendant around his neck, but Muros grabbed it first.

"No you don't!" he said. "I've seen how you touch it when you're around the myserae! It lets you control them, doesn't it?"

"Release me!" Vargas snarled. "The pendant was Hera's gift to my family!"

"What's yours is mine by right!" Muros gave a quick downward jerk, trying to break the chain. It held, though.

Then Vargas seized his wrist and squeezed hard, forcing his hand back inch by inch. The chamberlain's strength was incredible for a man his age. Muros gasped as his bones grated against each other, but he tightened his grip on the pendant. He wouldn't let an old man beat him.

He remembered a trick one of his swordsmanship instructors had taught him and suddenly jerked his arm upward, using the chamberlain's own strength as a weapon. Caught off balance, Vargas loosened his grip for an instant. Muros wrenched his hand free and felt the chain break. Shouting in triumph, he leaped back, holding the pendant out of reach.

At once the chamberlain seemed to wither like a flower too long without water. His shoulders hunched forward and his expression lost its sharpness. His eyes became weak and watery.

"Give it back," he said. "Give it to me, boy." Feebly, he tried to grab it.

"I've seen how you use it," Muros said, looking down at the pendant. "There's some sort of magic in it, isn't there? Well, you won't have it . . . not until you answer my questions!"

"They'll kill you," Vargas mumbled.

"What? Who will kill me? Speak up!"

Vargas raised his head. "My pets, of course. Yes, Jason

spoke truly. They *eat* people. They are savage, vicious monsters from the first days of the world. Are you happy knowing the truth? The pendant lets me control them, and it keeps them from preying on you and your people. Why do you think they've never raided your lands? If I don't have that pendant, they will devour us both!''

"Why didn't you tell me this before?'' Muros demanded.

"Because you're a fool!''

Muros bristled at that, but said nothing. He glanced down at the pendant, then back at his chamberlain, weighing the evidence. So many surprises—

"Give me my pendant!''

"How do I know you're telling the truth this time?'' Muros demanded.

"Look behind you.''

Muros turned. A myserae stood a hundred yards down the tunnel, watching them. Its eyes glowed a dull red. Slowly its beak began to move, opening and closing with little snapping sounds. Then it started toward them, gaining speed, like a wagon running out of control.

Muros swallowed, uneasy. He knew suddenly that Vargas had finally spoken the truth, that the myserae were beyond his control now, that this one would kill them both if he didn't do something.

"Give me the pendant—quickly!'' Vargas said.

Muros thrust it into his chamberlain's fumbling hands. Vargas touched it softly, almost reverently, and whispered something to it. It began to glow with a cold reddish light.

Muros looked up the tunnel. The myserae was still coming, its beak snapping, its wings flapping, its taloned feet clicking on the floor. It showed no sign of stopping. Fifty feet away and coming fast, then forty—

Muros drew his sword, suppressing his urge to run. It had been drilled into him a thousand times by his instructors. He crouched, blade ready. It wouldn't kill them without a fight.

Behind him, Vargas began to make a soft chirping sound.

The pendant suddenly pulsed with light, beating like a human heart. The light grew dazzling, almost blinding. Muros kept his gaze centered on the myserae. *Thirty feet—twenty—*

The creature began to slow, and as it slowed, it appeared to dissolve. Muros began to see the far end of the tunnel through its body. When it was fifteen feet away, it seemed as insubstantial as a ghost. Then Muros blinked and, just as suddenly, it was gone.

The light from the pendant faded. Muros stepped forward cautiously, examining the floor where the myserae had vanished. Not a trace of it remained.

Slowly he turned. He could feel sweat soaking his clothes and running down his back. He trembled, hardly able to breathe. Resheathing his sword, he leaned against the smooth, cool rock. He hadn't realized how truly terrified he had been until it was over.

"This way, Highness." Vargas indicated the crystal cavern again. He had regained all of his old composure.

"I'm sorry I doubted you," Muros said softly.

Vargas turned a cool, intense gaze on him. Only seconds ago, the chamberlain had been afraid of the myserae, Muros thought, and terrified of dying. Now, with the pendant returned, he had become cold and aloof once more. The talisman seemed to give him more than mere control over the myserae. He thought it made Vargas stronger both mentally and physically.

Taking a deep breath, Muros led the way forward. If Vargas had controlled the myserae for years, why hadn't he used them before? Why hadn't he seized control of the island? Why hadn't he forged an empire for himself?

And why didn't he stop the Argonauts from stealing my city and slaughtering my men?

Muros frowned. The more he thought of it, the more the old man's actions made no sense. He had the distinct impression that he had been lied to yet again.

They came to the mouth of the vast crystal cavern and Muros paused, gazing out at the dozens—perhaps hundreds—of myserae clustered there. Several flitted overhead from one side of the cavern to the other. Some pecked at the ground, or at each other, or groomed their leathery wings. The crystals writhed with reflections of movement.

"My friends . . ." Vargas whispered, clutching his pendant before him and moving forward among the creatures.

"Will you answer my questions now?" Muros asked, trying to sound properly cowed and humble.

Vargas stopped, as though considering the matter, then slowly looked back at him. "What do you want me to tell you?" He seemed grudging, as though reluctant to tell some great secret.

"Why didn't you stop the Argonauts before they attacked?"

"When Hera gave her first priest this pendant, she bade him use it to keep this island safe from all who would take it from her. It has many magical properties, but it cannot work miracles. Powerful gods watch over the Argonauts, Highness. If it had been within my power to destroy Prince Jason and his followers, I would have done so at once, for they are Hera's enemies. Only now, with the help of the myserae, can we hope to stop them."

"Why didn't you tell me this before?"

"Would you have believed me?"

Muros hesitated, then shook his head. "No." He knew he would have thought his chamberlain daft.

Vargas turned back to the myserae and began to chirp. Somehow the pendant's chain had become whole again; he pulled it over his head and settled it around his neck. It seemed to flicker with an inner light.

The myserae moved toward them, circling around. Muros felt a tremor of fear, but held himself still. The creatures seemed harmless now. As they chirped and chittered to Vargas, the crystals in the cavern caught the sound and carried it like the sweet song of a choir.

At last the chirping stopped. Muros looked expectantly at his chamberlain. "Well?" he said. "What now? Will they help us?"

"Yes," Vargas replied. "The time has come for our attack."

Two myserae shifted and moved forward. Each wore a small leather saddle strapped just above its wings. They knelt before the old man and waited calmly.

Muros glanced at his chamberlain, who only motioned him forward. Slowly, cautiously, Muros approached the first creature. It looked at him with its slitted red eyes, head tilted to one side as if studying him. Carefully he swung up into the saddle, wincing as a quick needle of pain shot through his ankle. His mount climbed to its feet and spread its wings, hopping forward impatiently.

"Whoa there!" he called, but it ignored him.

Vargas climbed onto the other myserae. He chirped to the rest, touching his pendant lightly with his right hand, and Muros watched the creatures line up two abreast behind them.

His myserae did not have reins or any way for him to hold on safely. How could he keep from falling off? He glanced at Vargas to see how he held on, and to his surprise, the chamberlain leaned forward and wrapped his arms around the myserae's neck.

Muros did the same. His skin crawled where it touched the creature. It trembled faintly beneath him.

As he tightened his grip, the myserae moved forward with a slow, swinging gait. Together they wove their way through the glittering spires of crystal, through the cavern and into another large tunnel that wound snakelike up through the mountain. As they progressed, the passageway occasionally widened into other caverns, but these were dark, with few crystals to light them. At other times, the tunnel narrowed and grew so low that the myserae had to duck its head.

Half an hour later, the cave's mouth appeared ahead of them. A cold, sharp wind blew steadily into the tunnel, and Muros could see the twilight sky. They had climbed nearly to the top of the mountain. A stunning view greeted him as his mount paused in the opening: two thousand rugged, rocky feet of mountain lay below them, full of scrub pines and gnarled, sickly yellow bushes. Below that lay a narrow, sandy beach, then the sea, darkening to deep blue-black farther out from shore. The sun, just settling beneath the distant horizon, capped the waves with gold and streaked the far sky with pinks and reds and yellows.

The cold air felt like a knife in his nose and lungs. His breath plumed before him. Looking left and right, he saw snow.

Slowly his myserae inched forward, and Vargas drew up next to him. "Hang on with both hands," the chamberlain told him.

"Why?" he asked, but as he did, his mount threw open its wings and dove forward, off the ledge.

The world fell out from under Muros, and they plummeted like a thousand pounds of rock. Gulping frantically, he gripped the myserae's neck so tightly his hands ached. They were falling—he weighed too much—they would smash on the rocks below—

Suddenly his myserae raised its wings, and with a small snapping sound, they caught the wind. The creature turned, soaring up and away into the air.

Muros pried one eye open. Below him, everything looked small, almost unreal. He had never been this high before. Slowly he began to breathe again.

Looking back, he found more of the myserae emerging from the mouth of the cave. They dove forward, catching the wind in their broad, leathery wings, taking flight after him by the dozens, then the hundreds.

Finally he spotted Vargas flying just above and to his

right. The old chamberlain gripped his mount strongly as the wind whipped through his hair and tunic. Slowly he raised one hand and pointed.

Muros saw his city just ahead. The *Argo* still sat at anchor, and dozens of people moved on the beach. In the last light of the day, they were loading chests onto the ship . . . *his* chests, things they had stolen from *his* palace. A blinding rage ran through him. How dare they rob him! How dare they steal his treasures! He would make them pay for that. Hercules and Jason would die for all the trouble they'd caused.

TWENTY

"THEY WILL COME," WITTA SAID.

Hercules frowned, feeling a growing impatience. Like all who spoke for the gods, Witta seemed to talk a lot but managed to say little. He had no patience for any of them.

"When?" Jason asked. "Today? Tomorrow?"

"Soon," she promised. "I can tell nothing more from the signs Athena sends me."

"Feh!" Hercules stepped out onto the balcony and stretched, looking up at the stars. The five of them had spent the last three hours in Muros's private suite: Jason, Theseus, Witta, Atalanta, and himself. It had been a council of war, but little had been accomplished.

Movement caught his eye and he turned, looking up, puzzled. A ripple of shadow moved across the constellations. A curtain of darkness fell across the moon. He blinked and it was gone.

"Jason. . . ." he said uneasily. "I think you better come here."

"Is something wrong?" Jason rose and hurried to his side.

"I don't know." He hesitated. "I think I saw something flying overhead . . . something big."

"What? The myserae?"

Atalanta called, "Myserae? Where?" In a second she had joined them, as had Theseus and Witta.

"Up there." Hercules pointed to the sky. "Something—perhaps many somethings—passed across the moon and the stars."

"The myserae!" Witta said. "They have come!"

"I didn't see what it was. Just . . . *blackness*."

Suddenly the air filled with darting movement as dozens of creatures flew into the courtyard. Cries of fear and alarm rang out from the palace gates and the city walls. Strange birdlike chirping noises echoed from the sky. Someone shouted, "To arms! We're under attack! To arms—" and then the warning ended in a brief, startled scream.

A myserae reared up before them, and the light spilling from the lamps in the room behind showed its red eyes and bloodstained beak. Setting its powerfully taloned feet on the balcony railing, it opened its maw and tried to slash Jason.

Darting forward, coming up under its left wing, Hercules seized its neck in both hands and twisted with all his might. Its wings pummeled him for a second; then he ripped out its throat with his bare fingers, spraying blood. The creature went limp. He heaved it over the railing and heard it hit the paving stones twenty feet below with a dull splat.

Jason and Theseus tore their swords from their scabbards. "We'll hold them here!" Jason called to him. "Get more weapons!"

"Right!" Turning, Hercules ran to the door. He heard

Atalanta following him. Quickly he surveyed the room but saw nothing useful, not a spear in the corner nor a sword on the wall. Just his luck—he hadn't thought it necessary to bring a spear to the meeting, and he knew Atalanta hadn't brought her bow, either.

The palace armory lay on the ground floor, he remembered. Side by side, they sprinted down the broad alabaster staircase, turned down the side corridor, and raced past the guardrooms. The armory door stood open, showing racks of spears, swords, bows, and arrows.

As Hercules took a double armful of spears, Atalanta helped herself to a pair of bows, strung them swiftly and slipped them over her right shoulder. Then she scooped up three quivers of arrows and a sword.

He didn't wait for her, but headed immediately back for the balcony. As he was halfway up the stairway, he heard her footsteps behind him. He hoped Jason and Theseus had been able to hold their own.

Jason and Theseus fought valiantly, but more and more of the myserae appeared on the balcony, pushing forward, beaks snapping. Jason's sword moved like an insect, darting here and there, drawing blood, slashing and parrying, digging deep into wings and chests. But it did no good. For every myserae that fell, two more waited to take its place.

Slowly they retreated through the doorway and into Muros's suite. Jason had just begun to think of trying to make it out into the hallway—few of the myserae would be able to get to them there—when Witta rushed past him, straight at the creatures.

She held a torch from the hall outside and waved it at the myserae, thrusting at first one, then another, of them. They drew back with hissing sounds.

"They fear the cleansing flame," Witta said. "They are creatures of darkness."

Hercules burst through the doorway, and Jason saw that

he carried perhaps two or three dozen spears. Hercules dropped them on the table, picked up the first, and threw it in a blur of speed. Like a pin through a piece of cloth, it pierced the nearest creature, which fell almost silently, feet and wings twitching.

Hercules threw two more spears, and then the other myserae turned, leaped from the balcony, and flew off into the darkness.

Cautiously, Jason moved forward, peering this way and that. Below, in the courtyard, he saw that several dozen men had rallied around Orestes. Together they formed a defensive ring, facing down perhaps thirty or forty of the creatures. Using spears and swords, they jabbed at several myserae that tried to attack from above. A few of the men held torches.

"They're afraid of fire!" Jason called down. "Get more torches!"

Orestes turned and barked orders to his men. Quickly they made their way to one of the guardhouses and pulled out a supply of fresh torches. As they lit them, a weird chirping noise started among the myserae, and a moment later, the creatures spread their wings and flew up to the walls and rooftops surrounding the courtyard.

"Kill them!" Muros demanded. He turned to look at Vargas. Their myserae perched atop the palace's east wall, looking down into the courtyard. He could not believe Vargas had called off the creatures' attack. Victory was in sight—why retreat?

"The myserae are more effective as instruments of fear," Vargas said as the myserae retreated, taking perches on rooftops and the city's wall, leaving tired, gasping men to lean on their swords and spears. "Besides, your people are among those below. Would you kill your own citizens?"

"No, of course not." Muros felt his face burning.

"Then let me handle them in my own way, Highness."

Muros gave a nod. "Very well." He didn't seem to have a choice.

He looked toward the balcony where Jason and Hercules had been fighting. They had vanished. If they got away because of Vargas—

Then Jason stepped out into the courtyard, calling something to the knot of men in a low voice. They began to retreat toward the doors to the palace, weapons ready.

Vargas clutched his pendant. "Wait!" he called, and his voice rolled like thunder throughout the courtyard. Everyone below paused, looking up.

"People of Sattis!" Vargas continued. "I am Vargas, chamberlain to His Eminence, King Muros. The king has returned this night to reclaim his lands. Throw down your weapons and you will be spared; keep them and my servants will rip you apart as surely as they will kill Prince Jason and his Argonauts. Sattis will be ours again this night!"

"Wait!" Jason cried, turning to face the crowd. "He's lying; I see no sign of King Muros! If we stand together, we can hold them off—"

"Your king lives!" Vargas screamed. "Look—even now he is beside me!"

He clutched his pendant again, and a dim red glow spread around him—around them both, Muros realized. He sat up straighter in his saddle, trying to look dignified and confident. "I am your king!" he shouted. "Put down your weapons, my friends! I have returned to free you from the Argonauts and their tyranny!"

As Muros watched, his people began to murmur excitedly among themselves.

"Throw down your weapons!" Muros called again. "The myserae obey my will! You will be spared . . . but only if you obey instantly!"

As he watched, his guardsmen hesitantly set their swords and daggers on the flagstones and backed away from them. Above, Vargas began to laugh, a high, quavering sound that set the king's skin a-crawl. At last, only a handful of men—all of them Argonauts—remained armed.

Vargas had been right, he realized. They had won! With only those few men, Jason couldn't hope to defend himself—let alone anyone else—against so many myserae!

He glanced toward the balcony where Jason and the others had been, but it was suddenly empty. Jason had fled. Chuckling, he knew it would not be long now. Vengeance was his!

"Now," he said, turning to Vargas, "kill them all!"

"As you command," Vargas said, and as he touched his pendant, the myserae began to stir on the walls around them.

"Slowly," Jason whispered to Orestes and the others outside, "move toward the door. As you get inside, run for the throne room. We'll rally there."

One by one, the remaining Argonauts began easing through the door and into the palace. Then a high whistle sounded and the myserae flew down at them like a pack of falcons unleashed, beaks snapping and talons outstretched.

"Run!" Jason shouted. He hurled Witta's torch at the closest myserae, which veered aside, throwing several other creatures off course. Orestes tumbled through the door last, and Jason slammed it shut, ramming the bolts home.

Hercules made a quick search of the antechamber. A three-inch-thick oak bar had been set out of sight behind a tapestry. He dragged it out, hefted it easily and slipped it between the door's large, intricately carved wooden handles.

"They won't get through *that* in a hurry," he said.

"Don't count on it," Jason told him. He could hear them moving outside, their clawed feet tapping on the flagstones. Something scratched on the door like a dog wanting in. He knew it wasn't a dog. "They'll break through whenever they're ready."

He pulled a torch from a wall sconce. It had almost gone out; he swung it over his head so it flared for a second, then burned with a steadier light.

"Has anyone got a plan?" Atalanta asked. She strung her bow and nocked an arrow, facing the door.

Everyone looked at Jason, even Theseus did.

"A plan . . ." Jason murmured. Then he grinned as he thought of Muros's own escape two days before. "Of course!"

The topmost panel of the door splintered suddenly. A myserae pecked at it, sending more splinters flying. It wouldn't hold much longer, Jason knew.

"Let me." Hercules stepped forward, set his feet wide apart and raised a spear over his head. The bronze point gleamed in the flickering light. Muscles cording like bands of iron in his neck and shoulders, he thrust forward. The spear pierced the creature's neck, then jerked free, spraying blood. A horrible, inhuman screaming sound came from outside. The doors shook, wood creaking, hinges groaning, as more of the creatures pounded on it, trying to break through.

"Hercules . . ." Atalanta said, shaking her head.

He turned to face her with an almost guilty expression. "Oops. That's two I owe you."

"You can argue about it later," Jason said, taking a quick head count. Twenty-one men out of his crew of forty-eight. Some would still be aboard the ship, he realized. Others would be in the city. Hopefully, they could get to safety before Muros's guards recovered their senses enough to arrest them . . . or the myserae struck.

"You're thinking of the secret passage!" Hercules said suddenly.

"Exactly. Follow me!" Jason bounded up the stairs two at a time, with Hercules and Atalanta right on his heels and the rest close behind.

Witta met him at the top. "This way," Jason said, turning and steering her back the way they had come. If that passage could whisk Muros to safety, it could do the same for them.

The main doors burst open just as they reached Muros's private chambers. Since they stood out of the myserae's line of sight, and the creatures weren't built for moving through the narrow confines of a building—even one as large as a palace—he thought they would be safe for a few minutes more.

He opened the door and motioned everyone though. After they were safely inside, Jason closed and barred it as securely as he could. Orestes and the others began piling furniture against it.

The secret panel had been boarded shut. Hercules crossed to it and began ripping the boards away one by one. Jason ran to the far wall and set fire to the huge, moldering old tapestries hanging there, hoping smoke and flames would confuse the myserae and give his band more time to get out of the city. Already he thought he heard creatures prowling the hallway outside.

When the entrance to the secret passage had been cleared, Hercules stood back. "You have the torch," he said.

Jason ducked through the opening and stood in the passageway for an instant, watching the torch's flame. It flickered in a sudden draft from the left. He knew they'd have to go in that direction to get out.

As he started forward, he called, "Stay close behind me, and watch your feet. There's no telling what's in here."

Testing each step before he took it, looking for traps in the walls, ceiling, and floor, he advanced with what seemed a snail's pace. His men followed in single file. Hercules brought up the rear, spear held ready.

*   *   *

"What do you mean, they've vanished?" King Muros demanded. He didn't understand how an army of myserae could miss twenty-odd warriors who had boarded themselves up somewhere inside his palace. As he paced the tower roof with nervous, frantic energy, he glared at Vargas. "Well?"

"Highness," Vargas sighed. "Whatever they have done, wherever they have gone, the myserae cannot find them. Perhaps they went into one of the secret passages."

Muros cursed himself for a fool. "Of course!" he said. "They saw the one in my chambers when you rescued me! They must have fled through it."

Vargas smiled a bit. "If so, they will be quite surprised. That particular passage has but three exits . . . and more than a hundred traps scattered through its length. There is only one safe path to any of the ways out." He chuckled. Muros didn't like the sound. "They will die soon enough if they tried to escape through that passage."

Muros snorted. "I'll believe they're dead when I see their bodies."

"Have you lost all your faith in me, Highness?"

"Humor me. You seem good at that."

The chamberlain frowned. "Very well," he said. "If you wish, I can send a couple of our friends to watch the exits. If the Argonauts and their men try to leave, they will be killed. Will that satisfy you?"

"Yes. Do it now, quickly!"

The chamberlain turned toward one of the waiting myserae and made a soft chirping sound, then whistled several times. When he touched the pendant around his neck, the creature turned and flapped off into the darkness.

When Muros looked up again, he saw flames dancing in the windows of several rooms in the east wing of his palace. He stared in horror. They had set fire to his private chambers! Everything—all his clothes and possessions— would be destroyed if he didn't do something. He gave a low moan of despair and grabbed Vargas's arm. "Look!"

"Please release me, Highness."

"But the fire!"

The chamberlain pulled away. "The myserae will be safe; they know enough to avoid the flames."

"Stop it!"

"How do you suggest? I can spit on it, if you wish. Otherwise . . ."

Muros cursed and ran to the edge of the roof. Twenty or so of his guards milled uselessly in the inner courtyard.

"You down there!" he called. They looked up at him blankly. "The east rooms are on fire! Get water and put out the flames, and call more people to help! Now *hurry*!"

When Muros turned and saw Vargas's mocking smile, he knew how helpless he'd become.

The tunnel wound deeper and deeper into the earth. Jason held up one hand and everyone behind him stopped. The floor ahead looked unusually smooth. He had already found two death traps—first a concealed pit with iron spikes at its bottom, and then a trapdoor that swung open over a hundred-foot drop into a dark pool of stagnant water—and he planned on taking no chances. He knelt and slowly ran his fingers across the stone.

Hercules pushed through the crowd behind him. "What is it?"

"A string," Jason said as he found it. Someone had stretched it an inch over the floor; in the dim light, it had been nearly invisible. He stood and stepped over it, then looked back. "Be careful."

Scowling, Hercules stepped back to make room for the other Argonauts. Atalanta took a large, exaggerated step over the string, and everyone followed her example. Hercules came last.

"What does it lead to?" he asked, studying the walls.

"I don't know. Want to find out?"

"Perhaps we should leave it for anyone following us."

"They probably already know it's here," Jason said.

He borrowed Hercules' spear, leaned forward and hooked the string from a safe distance. When he gave a gentle tug, the string came loose. He stood and looked at it more closely.

"It's rotted through on both ends. It wouldn't have hurt us."

Everyone laughed with nervous relief. Jason smiled and tossed the string over his shoulder.

"Come on," he said. "Let's get away from here."

He led them down the tunnel once more. Before they had taken thirty paces, a loud grating noise came from behind them, followed by an even louder *thump*.

They stopped and looked back. A huge slab of stone had fallen from the ceiling, completely blocking the passage. It would have killed most of them, Jason knew, if it had gone off as planned. He swallowed.

"At least," he said, "now we don't have to worry about anyone trying to follow us."

They continued in silence.

Many hours later, the tunnel leveled off and Jason smelled the briny tang of the sea. He motioned for the others to stop. They would have to go even more cautiously now in case King Muros had arranged an ambush for them.

He had found nearly a dozen death traps after the trip string. Some released iron spikes from the walls and ceiling; others dropped stone blocks, and one even would have sent a volley of arrows down the length of the tunnel, if the bowstrings hadn't rotted through years before. Anyone less careful might have been killed several times over.

Ahead, the tunnel seemed to open into a larger room—perhaps the cave Hercules had spotted the day before? Jason strained to hear and was almost certain he detected the sounds of low surf.

"Keep alert," he said. "I think the exit is just ahead."

Hercules hefted his spear, Atalanta readied her bow, and everyone else except Witta raised swords. Jason started forward more slowly than ever.

Sure enough, the tunnel opened into a natural cavern; he wondered at the curved white-limestone ceiling high overhead and the stalactites and stalagmites all around them. The air was thick and heavy with moisture. Somewhere close, water dripped.

The breeze grew stronger now. The torch in his hand flickered, throwing wild shadows, and in more than a few of the shadows, Jason thought he saw tiny yellow eyes peering out. Probably bats, he decided. He saw nothing to alarm him, though, so he continued down the path a bit faster.

Here and there, the floor had been leveled by human hands, he saw, noting the marks of chisels where limestone flows had been cut away. Then abruptly the path dropped six inches, and sand crunched under his feet.

Ahead, through the mouth of the cave, he glimpsed open water. He began to breathe more easily. The morning twilight had begun, purpling the night sky. They had made it.

A half-hour hike down the beach, he figured, and they would be at the ship. Once they rescued anyone left in Sattis and found their way aboard the *Argo*, they would be sailing again.

Smiling at the thought, he lowered his torch, planning to grind it into the sand so it wouldn't be seen by anyone outside. A few men behind him laughed with nervous relief.

Then a myserae flew into the cave and landed before him. He froze, staring up into its red eyes. Before it could strike, he whipped up the torch and thrust it at the creature's eyes. It gave a sharp whistle and hopped back a foot, then let loose a grating shriek as it attacked.

TWENTY-ONE

TOWARD DAWN, KING MUROS STAG-gered out onto the city walls and collapsed, weeping. Soot caked his face and hands and clothes, but he barely noticed. Blisters covered his hands and face, but he barely felt them.

Far off, he thought he heard his chamberlain laughing. Even when he pressed his hands over his ears, he still heard the sound.

The immensity of this night's disaster overwhelmed him. His palace was all but gone, consumed by flames, and the fire had spread to the city. To the west, the gran-aries now blazed like torches. To the east, the merchants' quarter smoldered, reduced to ashes and gutted shells of buildings. To the north and south, dozens of new fires had broken out. Everywhere he looked, he saw smoke and flame and utter ruin.

And bodies—bodies everywhere too. He winced and

pulled his gaze from the streets, where corpses lay in ragged heaps.

He and his men had almost gotten the palace fire under control toward midnight. Long lines of men and women from the city had assembled, and they had passed water up from the wells and the river in pails, jars, and wooden bowls—anything and everything helped. His guards emptied them onto the flames by the hundreds, then the thousands.

Unfortunately, the myserae chose that very moment to fall on his city like a pack of starving wolves, snatching men from the wells, guards from the courtyards, and even children from the roofs of houses where they sat watching the disaster unfold. Hundreds, perhaps thousands, had died in the space of ten minutes, and then the myserae began to devour their victims.

Those who managed to flee indoors might have thought themselves lucky, but while the myserae lingered in the streets, the fire in the palace flared anew and rapidly spread. Muros had watched, helpless, as it consumed building after building in the palace complex, then leaped the walls and started on the city around them.

If a thousand died in the myserae's attack, five times that many must have perished, trapped indoors as the flames raged through the city.

And Muros—still atop the palace wall, left alone by the myserae for some reason—could only watch the horrors unfolding below. He had screamed for Vargas to call off his creatures, and he had screamed to the myserae, and finally he had screamed to the gods. And when no answer came and the wind blew the stench of death and burning human flesh to him, he had retched until he thought he would die himself, so great was his agony.

And through it all, Vargas was nowhere to be found.

When Vargas finally appeared, hours later, the slaughter was done. The myserae had fed, and taking wing, they soared high over the city, their raw voices filling the night with harsh cries.

"I am sorry, Highness," Vargas had said. "I don't know what came over them. I will send them away."

Muros trembled. Send them away? What good could that possibly do now, when all his city had been ruined? If Vargas hadn't still been sitting on one of the creatures, Muros knew he would have killed him on the spot . . . with his bare hands, if he had to.

Vargas touched the pendant around his neck, closed his eyes, and in a few seconds most of the myserae took wing, heading west, back to their mountain home. Perhaps a dozen remained, and they flew down and settled along the palace walls to either side. Blood stained their beaks and feathers and feet, Muros saw with a shudder. The creatures began to preen themselves almost gaily.

"These should be enough to guard your city," Vargas said.

"Guard it from what?"

Vargas nodded toward the sea. Slowly Muros turned, gazing out through a haze of smoke. The eastern sky had begun to pale with the coming dawn. Now he could see what his chamberlain meant: the *Argo* gently rolled with the waves fifty yards out from shore.

"Jason—" he gasped.

"No, Highness. A few of his Argonauts were drinking in the city taverns when we attacked. They rallied and made it back to their ship even as our myserae drove Jason and the others to their death in the tunnels below."

Muros relaxed a little. He could take some comfort in that, he thought. With Jason dead, at least he had his revenge.

He heard a flutter of wings, and when he whirled, Vargas and the rest of the myserae had flown off. They circled several times, then disappeared into the smoke. He did not know where they had gone, nor did he care.

"I'm well rid of you," he muttered. "May you never return, Vargas, for if you do, I'll cut off your head and mount it over the city gates!"

TWENTY-TWO

JASON SHOVED HIS TORCH AGAIN AND
again at the myserae's face. The creature jerked back like a puppet on a
string, making unhappy snaps with its beak. Flapping its
wings, it lifted off the ground, reaching with its claws.

Jason leaped forward, sword swinging. Behind him, he
heard the sharp twang of Atalanta's bow, and an arrow
suddenly struck the creature's left wing. With a snap of
its beak, it broke the arrow off. A trickle of blood ran
from the wound. Opening its beak, it hissed in anger,
showing a forked yellow tongue.

"Circle around it," Hercules called. "We can kill it
easily enough!"

Around him, the Argonauts divided forces rapidly. Hercules and Theseus led half the group to the right while
Orestes and Meleagar led the rest to the left. Jason kept
dancing forward with his torch, keeping the creature confused and off balance. Once he saw that they had it ringed

in, he called, "Attack! We've got it now!"

Everyone began shouting, taunting, poking it with swords and spears so it didn't know which way to turn or who to attack next. Atalanta put a dozen arrows into its chest, and it screamed and hissed and snapped, just barely keeping them at bay.

Finally, squawking in pain and frustration, it darted toward the mouth of the cave, trying to escape. Jason circled around, keeping his torch in its face.

"Can I borrow your sword?" he heard Hercules ask someone.

Theseus replied, "Gladly!"

And an instant later, Hercules leaped forward and took a hard swing at the creature's left leg. The sword bit halfway through, stuck for a moment, then came free. The myserae stopped and whined, a sound that chilled Jason. It tried to put weight on that wounded leg, stumbled, and went down.

Lowering his torch, Jason watched as the others leaped forward, hacking wildly at its head and wings and chest. At last it lay in a puddle of its own blood, wings twitching faintly, beak opening and closing by reflex.

"Ahem!" Atalanta said loudly. He glanced up to find her staring at Hercules, arms crossed, a look of mock severity on her face.

"Oops," Hercules said almost guiltily. "But surely this one didn't count—"

"The *next* monster, you said!"

Jason chuckled. It seemed their friendly rivalry would never end.

"How about the next *four*?" Hercules offered. "I really don't think this one should count, but—"

"Four it is," Atalanta said.

"You know," Jason told her, "you're going to end the quest with Hercules owing you more monsters than there are in the world, if you're not careful."

She made a face. "Don't remind me!"

"It *wasn't* my fault!" Hercules protested.

"Cover me?" Jason said to her.

"Gladly," she replied, giving Hercules a triumphant look, and she nocked another arrow as she joined Jason.

After setting his torch in the sand so nobody on the beach would see it, Jason stole softly from the cavern's mouth. He kept a careful watch on the sky, but nothing moved there. Nor did there seem to be any guards—human or otherwise—within sight. The myserae they had killed must have been a lone sentry, he realized. He relaxed a little and motioned for everyone to join him.

"Look," Atalanta said, pointing to the east.

Jason whirled, hand dropping to the hilt of his sword. Toward the city, he saw a faint orange glow lighting the sky. It had to be a fire. Then he began to smile. The fire he had started must have gone out of control and burned down most of the palace.

"A fire might provide enough confusion for us to reach the *Argo*," Theseus said.

"We'll have to hurry," Hercules said. "Day will soon be upon us. We don't want Muros or his guards—or the myserae—to spot us on the beach when we get there."

Jason sheathed his sword. "Then we'll hurry," he said.

Turning, he jogged up the beach, leading the way along the firm sand near the water's edge. Everyone followed him. He tried to keep a steady pace, but every so often he paused to let Witta and Theseus and the other stragglers catch up, and they caught their breath for a few minutes before pressing on.

The sun had already broken over the horizon as they rounded a small jut of land and came into sight of the city. The first thing Jason noticed was the fire—the whole city seemed ablaze, from one end to the other. Dozens of men and women had taken refuge on the beach, huddling behind the fishing boats drawn up on the shore. There didn't seem to be any guards among them . . . or any myserae, he saw with relief. They also didn't seem to be armed.

He turned his attention to the docks, which were empty, then gazed beyond to the *Argo*. His ship lay safe at anchor a hundred yards out from shore. He spotted Orpheus and Telamon on lookout in the bow. Two myserae lay on the deck, their bodies full of arrows, and several more bodies floated in the water. His men hadn't been caught off guard, it seemed. Closing his eyes, he breathed a silent prayer of thanks to Poseidon.

"There's one!" a voice called.

Jason turned to face Hylas. The boy was pointing at the sky, where a pair of myserae circled high above.

"We've no time to waste," Jason said grimly. "We'll take one of the fishing boats. Hercules, Orestes, Theseus—find one."

The three men jogged over to the nearest boat. At their approach, the refugees there scrambled away. Hercules, using his immense strength, dragged the boat to the water. It would take two trips, Jason realized, to get them all to the *Argo*. He hesitated, then decided to try it.

"Hercules, you man the oars," he said as he helped Witta aboard. Then he named Atalanta and half of his men, and they seated themselves inside. He and Orpheus pushed them out into the water, and Hercules began rowing swiftly out toward the ship.

Jason kept an eye on the myserae overhead. Two more joined the first pair, and they began to circle lower.

"Maybe we had best swim to the *Argo*," Theseus suggested. "It is not far, and the creatures might hesitate to attack us if we are in the water."

Jason thought about it for half a second, then nodded. "Hurry!" he said. "We'll swim for it!"

Quickly they stripped down to their undergarments. Meleagar and Theseus dove into the water first and began swimming strongly. The others followed.

Jason went last, wading out into the cool water, grip-

ping his sword in both hands and watching the sky. He
would hold on the weapon until everyone was swimming,
he decided, in case the myserae attacked.

Hearing a low, croaking whistle, Jason glanced to his
left. Another myserae had appeared. Wings spread wide,
it glided a foot over the waves, clawed feet dangling. It
planned to snatch one of them from the water, he realized.

He began to splash, hoping to attract its attention, and
sure enough, it veered toward him. As it neared, its talons
began to reach for him.

Jason ducked down. At the last possible moment, he
thrust his sword upward as he pushed off with his legs,
and he caught the creature in the belly, opening a long,
deep cut that spilled its inner organs and a shower of
blood. Then the creature hit the water, flopped and floun-
dered, and began to make a desperate shrieking sound.

That seemed enough to discourage the rest of the myserae. They circled high overhead, but made no attempts
to stop them.

Dropping his sword, Jason continued to swim out to
the *Argo*. In a few minutes he reached it, pulled himself
up using one of the dangling ropes, and stood shivering
on the deck.

"We made it," Hylas said, as if he scarcely believed
it himself.

Jason gazed across at the city. The fire still burned out
of control, and a thick black column of smoke rose toward
the heavens. When one of the palace roofs collapsed and
flames leaped hundreds of feet into the air, he knew the
fire would have to burn itself out; nobody could stop it
now.

Telamon offered him a towel, which he accepted grate-
fully. Thinking of King Muros, his smile broadened as he
began to dry himself off. He was laughing a minute later.

"What's so funny?" Hercules demanded.

"We've burned the palace, looted the treasury, and

forced Muros to claim help from the myserae . . . and he's going to think he *won*!''

"Muros did not win," Orpheus said darkly.

Jason looked at him. "What do you mean? Is he dead?"

"I'm not sure. All I know is that the myserae attacked everyone, not just us. As we fought our way out of the city, we saw them feeding on hundred of Muros's own people."

Jason shuddered at the thought. "A horrible fate."

"Then it's not a victory for any of us," Hercules said. "But this isn't over yet, Jason. We have to finish it. We have to destroy the myserae."

"All in good time," Jason said slowly. He studied the palace as a new plan began to form in his mind. Perhaps Muros had lost control of his creatures. Or perhaps feeding the myserae had been part of the unholy bargain Muros had made to gain their help.

It didn't matter. Muros had written his death sentence long before that. *For now,* Jason thought, *let Muros believe he has won.* They would sail around the island, he decided. The myserae would see them leave. King Muros would let down his guard. And then the Argonauts would return by night to strike again. . . .

"Raise the anchor and hoist the sails!" he called, and as his men ran to obey, he began to tell Hercules, Theseus, and Witta what he had in mind.

"And this time," he vowed, "King Muros will tell us the truth of where to find the myserae!"

"And then?" Hercules said.

"We kill him," Jason said grimly.

TWENTY-THREE

MUROS WADED THROUGH KNEE-deep piles of ash in the courtyard as he headed for what remained of the throne room. His guards had concentrated their efforts on saving this portion of the palace before the myserae attacked, and as a result, it was less severely burned than any other. It actually had *walls*, though the roof had collapsed. Sodden ash and half-burned beams littered the floor.

The throne, however, remained intact and upright. He brushed it off, sat down and leaned his head in his hands.

Footsteps sounded outside. Muros froze, a tremor of fear running through him. Was it Vargas, returning to gloat, or one of the myserae, come to devour him as its kin had devoured nearly all his people?

A man in a bloodstained guard's uniform appeared. He seemed dazed. He stared at Muros for a long moment, a confused look on his face.

"What is your name?" Muros demanded after a minute.

"Alimos, Highness," the man whispered.

"Are there any more of my guards alive?"

"A few, Highness—we are searching the city for survivors now . . ."

"How many of my people are left?"

"Highness . . ."

Muros snapped, "How many, I said!" Alimos winced. "None, Highness . . . they're gone."

"Gone?" Muros blinked. "What do you mean, gone? Surely the fire and the myserae didn't kill them all. *You're* still here, after all. And you said there were other guards—"

The man shrugged helplessly. "They fled during the night. I would have, too, if not for my oath."

Muros nodded. "Well done," he said. "Are any officers left?"

"No, Highness. At least, none that I saw."

"Then a promotion is in order." Muros rose, and Alimos cringed a little. "You are my new Captain of the Guard!" Muros said. "Find the other guards and bring them here. We have work to do."

"C-Captain of the Guard? *Me?*"

"There doesn't seem to be anyone else," Muros said dryly. "And I always reward loyalty."

"Highness!" He looked down, blushing, and Muros wondered if he had made a mistake. No, he told himself, he needed a Captain of the Guard, and there didn't seem to be anyone else.

"You have your job," he said. "Get on with it!"

"Thank you!" Alimos bowed, then began to back from the room.

"Wait!" Muros called. He found himself gripping the arms of his throne so hard his fingers hurt. The Argonauts might well be the greatest remaining danger. "What of the *Argo*?" he asked. "Is it still here?"

"No, Highness. They're gone as well. They sailed with the morning light."

Muros sank back. A weight had been lifted from him. Without the Argonauts, without the myserae, he would be able to rebuild.

"Very well," he said. "You may go."

"Yes, Highness!" Alimos bowed, ducked out through the door, and Muros heard him running.

Then a slight footstep sounded behind him. He jumped in surprise, but it was only Vargas. Muros glared at him. An hour ago, he would have launched himself at the man's throat, but now all his energies seemed spent. He wanted nothing more than to wake up and find the last two days had been only a horrible dream.

A pair of myserae glided in and landed on the wall, perching there like prize falcons. They chirped and whistled to Vargas, who stroked his pendant and answered in their language.

"Send your creatures away," Muros told him.

But Vargas said, "They must protect us, Highness."

"The Argonauts are gone."

"But I fear for your life. Your people are not happy, Highness. They might rise against you."

Muros gave a bitter laugh. "What people? I have only seen one other man this day. The rest have fled."

"No, Highness, there are more out there hiding. They fear for their lives, so they do not show themselves. I sense the beating of many hearts, and I feel the hatred within them. They blame you for what happened. They will kill you, if you don't take precautions."

"Let them kill me," Muros said. "I have nothing left to live for." He felt a numb heaviness inside, and he realized he really *didn't* care if he lived or died. Everything he had ever known, everything he had ever loved, had been destroyed. His palace, his city, his people . . . nothing mattered anymore.

"Surely you don't mean that, Highness."

Muros stared at him. "No," he said softly, "you're right, Vargas. I don't want to die yet." Not with so much left undone, he told himself. He still needed revenge, and not only against the Argonauts. Or the myserae. He narrowed his eyes as he studied his chamberlain. The old man seemed to be smiling as he stroked his pendant.

It's all your fault, Vargas, he thought. *Soon you will have to send the last of your myserae away. And then I will kill you myself.*

The thought gave him little comfort.

TWENTY-FOUR

J ASON SAILED NORTH, SLOWLY TURN-
ing northwest as they followed the
coast, passing small deserted-looking
fishing villages. From the size of the Isle of Sattis, he
knew it would take most of the day to circle all the way
around, assuming favorable winds, of course.

Most of the crew had retired below to sleep and rest,
but he lingered in the bow, staring at the passing shore.
On this side of the island, level ground made for good
farmland. They passed fields of wheat and rye and other
grains, olive and apple orchards, and lush pastures where
sheep and goats and cattle grazed. Word must have spread
about the disaster in the city, for he saw few people. It
was just as well; if he didn't see them, neither would the
myserae.

Witta joined him as noon approached. He gave her a
brief nod.

"You should rest," she said.

"Soon," he promised.

The priestess chuckled humorlessly. "I had a dream," she said, "and my dreams always come true."

"What did you dream?"

"Once more I saw the man who controls the myserae . . . a priest of Hera. He has a silver pendant. When we take it, his power over the myserae will be gone."

"Will he be there tonight?"

Slowly she shook her head. "I don't know. That was not part of my dream."

Jason turned, letting his gaze sweep from the farmlands to the hills and mountains. The myserae lived somewhere on Sattis, he told himself. But where?

Toward midnight they reached the city again. Hercules and Orestes lowered the *Argo*'s two boats, and Jason's men began climbing into them. Jason took his place in the stern of Hercules' boat. Witta came last and sat next to him. Something white glimmered in her hands, and it took Jason a minute to realize it was a wand. He swallowed a little uneasily. *More magic.*

The mooring lines were released and the rowers bent to their task, Hercules in this boat, Orpheus and Ilios in the other.

For a moment, Jason turned and looked back at his ship. The six men he had left there scarcely seemed enough.

"Do not worry," Witta whispered to him. "Athena is with us."

"I hope she knows what she's doing," he murmured.

"She is a powerful goddess."

His city resembled a mausoleum more than anything else, King Muros thought. It now held far more corpses than living people.

Over the day, people began to straggle in, as Vargas had predicted. A few guards, dozens of commoners . . .

they all headed to him, looking for him to save them. For him to tell them what to do.

He had sent them out to the countryside. It would take years to rebuild the city. They would be better off starting anew a bit farther down the coast, he thought.

So he sat alone in all the city, reclining in his throne, a small amphora of summer wine in one hand. At least his cellars had been spared. Tilting the vessel back, he drank until even the dregs were gone. Then he dropped the amphora and heard it clink against the other empty ones already on the floor. He winced, swore, and picked up a fresh one. After pulling out the wax stopper with his teeth, he took a long swallow.

His fault. It had all been his fault—the Argonauts capturing Sattis, the myserae killing his people.

He wept. How could he have been so stupid? How could he have listened to Vargas? How had he let his lands, his life, be destroyed?

He hated Vargas. Again and again he vowed to find the old man and kill him, despite his myserae guards. But he lacked the force of will to do anything about his hatred. Instead, he mumbled curses to himself, and drank, and cried for what might have been.

At last he heard noises. Screams, he thought with a giggle. Dimly, he looked up. The room flickered around him like a candle in the wind. The jar slipped from his fingers, spilling wine all over his clothes, but he scarcely noticed.

Screams? He was certain he'd heard screams.

He got to his feet unsteadily and staggered toward the once majestic staircase. It ended halfway up, and ashes covered it, and the unburied corpse of a guard lay spread-eagled in its center like one last grisly ornament.

The world blurred and twisted around him as he moved, the shadows distorted, a dull roar filling his head. *My fault. All my fault.* He seemed to be walking in a dream. Somehow he found himself on the palace walls, looking out at the burned-out remains of his city. The world swayed and he caught his balance against the battlements.

The screaming started again, but it was distant, muted. As he watched, a pair of myserae descended on a fat old man who had been cautiously picking his way down the street. Beaks snapping like butcher's knives, clawed feet ripping, they tore him apart. Blood spurted high in the air, but Muros turned away and continued his walk as though he hadn't seen anything unusual.

The stone statues of the gods, facing the central courtyard, seemed to move as he passed them. They laughed and beckoned to him.

"You are the greatest fool of all," Hera said with a laugh.

"Your father weeps for you," Hades told him.

"The light is coming soon," Athena whispered.

He pressed his hands over his ears as he wandered on. He did not want to hear them. He did not want to remember any more.

After that, his mind wandered for a time. He played games with the statues, tag and catch-me and hide-and-seek. He felt free and happy with them, and safe, so safe. He never wanted to leave.

But at last he grew aware of himself once more, and he found himself back in his throne room. A solitary torch guttered in its sconce in the far wall; he could barely see by its dim, uncertain light. Throwing himself onto his throne, he reached for another jar of wine, but the crate was empty. He had drunk the last of it.

His stomach began to heave, but there was nothing inside him except emptiness. He choked, coughed, spat, and felt no better. He sank back, eyes closed, and again he lost track of the world.

When he next looked up, he found Vargas standing there, waiting for him. The old man was laughing soundlessly and clutching the pendant around his neck. Without thinking, Muros tried to draw his sword, but he couldn't seem to find its hilt. He lunged at the chamberlain anyway, trying to grab him by the throat, and as he leaped, he seemed to hang in the air for an eternity. Then Vargas knocked him down and kicked him in the face, still laughing.

"Why?" Muros asked, whimpering. "Why?"

"The time for your people is over, Highness." Vargas advanced on him. Muros cringed. "My myserae have all stretched their wings, and it felt *good*. Serving you made them hunger, and their hunger had to be fed. Soon they will start to breed again, for the first time in a thousand years, and the skies will grow dark with their multitudes!"

Muros crawled over to a corner and curled into a ball. He tried to shut out Vargas's voice. He could still hear the statues calling to him. He could still hear laughter. He could still hear the screams of his people.

He began to whimper again.

As Jason walked through the dark, corpse-filled streets of the city, he grew more uneasy. A deep, unnatural silence stretched around him. Not a bird, not an insect, made a noise.

Even without the bodies, you could tell that something terrible had happened here. The atmosphere reeked of despair. Almost unconsciously, he moved closer to Hercules, drawing comfort from his friend's presence.

"The myserae," Hercules said suddenly, "destroyed Muros's own people." His voice sounded odd and out of place in the quiet.

"For some reason, Muros let them do it," Jason said. He felt a deep disgust for the young king and knew again that he couldn't leave this land without seeing Muros dead.

The only light in the whole city shone from the palace. No one manned the battlements, and the gates stood wide open, as if Muros expected them. Jason hesitated. A trap?

"Wait here," he said to his men, and then he motioned

for Hercules, Atalanta, and Theseus to advance with him.

Slowly they crept forward to investigate. Hercules and Atalanta drifted from shadow to shadow so stealthily that at times Jason lost track of them. They all reached the gates together and slipped into the courtyard.

Turning, Jason prowled forward, searching for any signs of guards or myserae. The light, he saw now, came from the throne room.

"There is no one on guard," Atalanta whispered. "I think I can hear someone talking inside, though."

Jason nodded grimly. If Muros was stupid enough to give the Argonauts a chance to enter the city by surprise, they certainly intended to use it to their advantage.

He motioned for his men, and swiftly they all joined him.

"Ready?" he asked. Nods came from all around.

Atalanta turned to Hercules. "Remember your promise this time," she cautioned.

Hercules grinned. "Of course. The first *four* myserae are yours."

"And don't forget it this time!"

The next time Muros looked up, Vargas had been joined by eight myserae. Shadows covered the old man's face, making him look . . . not sinister, but hollow, as if his body were a shell with nothing human left inside.

Vargas laughed harshly. "I wanted to see your death," he said. "I wanted to savor it. That's why I saved you for last."

Muros just looked at him.

"Come now, surely you won't disappoint me. Aren't you going to beg for your life, my pretty little pet?"

"Is that all I was to you?" Muros heard himself ask.

"You were less than that. A pet I might feel something for. You were a fool, a means to an end. Hera promised me power in return for serving her, and power I have!"

When Muros said nothing, Vargas snarled, "Your

death has come. Save your breath for the afterworld.'' He stepped forward, raising his hands toward the pendant.

There was a low whistle, then a solid *thunk*. Vargas staggered, a startled expression on his face. He looked down.

The tip of an arrow protruded three inches from his chest. Blood gushed from the wound, staining his white tunic. He opened his mouth as if to speak, but a pink foam streamed from his lips. Suddenly he forced himself upright, one hand tightening on the pendant around his neck. With a gurgling sound, he turned. Eight inches of wood, with bright yellow-and-blue fletching, stuck out from his back like a banner.

Stunned, Muros looked at the doorway. There stood Jason, Hercules, Atalanta, and many more Argonauts. But hadn't they gone? Hadn't they sailed off in their ship? How was this possible?

''That's one!'' Hercules said.

''A man doesn't count as a monster!'' Atalanta protested. ''And he isn't even dead!''

''A mere technicality . . .'' Hercules said with a grin.

''Kill them!'' Vargas shouted to his creatures, blood spraying from his lips. He staggered toward his myserae. ''Kill them!''

Seven of the eight myserae trembled. Six turned toward the Argonauts while the other one, beak snapping, faced Muros.

Muros covered his head, suddenly afraid to die. Then the statue-gods surrounded him once more, comforting him, taking his hands and pulling him gently toward them.

Laughing, Muros went away. He did not look back.

''They're all yours!'' Hercules said to Atalanta.

''I only want four of them,'' she said, nocking another arrow and letting it fly. It struck the nearest myserae in the left eye; quivering, the creature collapsed. ''You and the others can have the rest.''

"Generous of you."

Jason threw a spear at the myserae closest to Muros, striking the creature's head and glancing off, distracting it for a second. Hissing, it turned to face him. Behind him, the others let loose their shots. Spears and arrows flew through the air, striking the myserae. Two more of them collapsed, and a third threw back its head with a high-pitched keening sound.

As Jason took a defensive stance, one of Atalanta's arrows hit the myserae about to attack him, followed a second later by another arrow. The creature collapsed, twitching.

Unfortunately, that had given Vargas time to climb onto the myserae that had stayed behind. Jason leaped forward, but too late—flapping its powerful wings, the creature took to the air. In seconds, it vanished across the ruined palace.

Jason turned to face the three remaining myserae. Hercules threw his second spear in a blur of motion. Beside him, Atalanta fired another pair of shots from her bow. Two more myserae fell.

"That's one for me," Hercules said, grinning.

"And *three* for me." Atalanta aimed again, fired twice in quick succession and shouted, "Four!"

Hercules grinned. "Finally!" he cried.

Suddenly the fight was over. All the myserae had fallen. Several still twitched faintly, so the Argonauts moved among them, thrusting their swords through the creatures' heads to make certain they were dead. No one moved to reclaim the spent arrows or spears. Hercules found he didn't blame them; the whole room had an unclean atmosphere. He wanted nothing so much as to rush out and wash himself all over.

King Muros cowered, screaming mindlessly, his arm covering his head. Jason jogged up the steps to the throne and pulled him to his feet. Muros's teeth chattered, but he stopped screaming. His eyes rolled wildly. He began to drool.

"He's gone mad," Jason said, sounding disgusted.

"Can you blame him?" Theseus asked in soft tones.

Jason pushed Muros away. The king collapsed on the floor in a disjointed heap, whimpering like a sick puppy.

"Look at him," Hercules said, feeling sick. All his pent-up hatred was suddenly gone, turned to pity. It seemed that Muros hadn't been responsible; the other man was, the one Atalanta had shot, the one who wore the pendant.

"The gods have touched his mind," Jason said softly. "Could you kill him as he is now?"

Hercules put down his sword and went to Muros. He shook the younger man's shoulder gently, but Muros only whimpered.

"Vargas!" Muros cried suddenly. "Not the mountain, Vargas! Not the mountain!"

"But *which* mountain?" Jason said grimly. "Let's get back to the ship." He did not look at Muros.

As they left the city, something made Jason glance back. A few fires still burned here and there, but most of the damage was done. Little remained standing.

A lone figure appeared silhouetted atop the city's highest wall. It had to be Muros, he thought.

As he watched, Muros, King of Sattis, leaped from the battlements, plunged down, and vanished from sight.

Jason winced. It seemed that King Muros had found a measure of strength in his insanity after all. He felt nothing but pity for the young king now. Clearly, this Vargas had been the one responsible . . . the one who had controlled the myserae and caused all the problems on Thorna.

TWENTY-FIVE

ITTA SANK TO HER KNEES BE-
fore the small altar to Athena
that she had built in her cabin
with Theseus's help. She felt a gathering presence almost
before she'd closed her eyes, almost before she'd driven
all thoughts of the material world from her mind.

Before her, on the altar, lay a white gull that one of the
Argonauts had caught for her.

"I offer this beast to Pallas Athena, who watches over
me and my people," she cried in a singsong voice. "May
she guide us and strengthen us in our time of need."

Using a small bronze knife, she slit the gull's throat,
and as its blood poured out, she caught it in a wooden
bowl.

The feeling of a presence, of a gathering power, grew
stronger. *It's just like the time Athena spoke to me at
home, on Thorna!* she thought with excitement.

The gull moved its head. Its green eyes turned blood

red as it sat up and spread its wings. Then it hissed at her.

Witta felt her heart flutter. This was magic, but slightly different from what had happened back home . . . an angry, bitter magic. Suddenly she felt very, very afraid.

"Priestess," the bird said in a woman's scornful voice, "you have helped destroy those I hold dear. You have aided Hercules and the other Argonauts. You have flaunted my power as Queen of the Gods—"

"Hera!" Witta cried.

The gull's beak twisted back in a cruel smile. "So you know my name, dear."

Witta swallowed. "I summon Pallas Athena!" she cried again. "I invoke the name of the goddess I serve! Aid me, Athena, in my time of need!"

The bird twisted on the altar. One eye turned gray, then the other. The atmosphere in the room changed a little, and Witta felt it. Hera had gone.

The gull preened itself for a moment, then looked at her.

"Athena?" she asked softly.

"Witta," Athena's voice said from the bird. "There is a mountain ahead of you. Watch for its evil face. That is where the myserae dwell."

The gull fell back and began to writhe on the table. One eye turned red. It hissed, "Turn them back or I will see you all dead! *Dead!* And all your people back home on Thorna! Do you hear me, Priestess? Do you hear me—"

And just as suddenly as it had begun, the magic ended. Witta felt the presences vanish, and for several minutes she sat alone before the small wooden altar, shivering a little.

Finally she covered the gull, finished her prayers, and rose to tell Jason what she had learned. She could not let Hera intimidate her. Athena would protect her.

A mountain with an evil face, though . . . she did not

know what that meant, but she trusted her goddess. Everything would become clear when the proper time came.

Hercules frowned thoughtfully as Witta recited her tale. In addition to Hercules, Jason had called Theseus, Orestes, and Atalanta his cabin to hear it.

"A mountain with an evil face," Hercules said again. "I don't remember seeing anything like that, do you, Atalanta? Not even when we sailed around the island."

"No." She chewed her lower lip thoughtfully. "But then, we weren't looking for a face, either."

"I feel it's safe to assume that this mountain lies well beyond the point we reached by chariot," Jason said, spreading out on the table the map Theseus had found earlier. He stabbed the middle of the island with one finger. "That's where we stopped. The mountains continue unbroken all the way to the westernmost tip of Sattis, so this 'evil face' could be anywhere. However, I think the myserae must be on the very last mountain. That's why Muros and his people never saw them. It would be an easy flight to Thorna."

Witta hesitated. "But the face . . ."

"A statue?" Hercules suggested. "Or something carved into the mountainside?"

"It's possible," Jason said. "Did Athena say anything else that might be helpful?"

Witta said, "Only to watch for an evil face."

"We must trust Athena," Theseus said, looking at each of them in turn, "as we have always trusted our gods to guide us to success."

They sailed up the coast slowly, passing empty beaches, desolate cliffs, barren lands. The mountains remained steep and jagged, almost forbidding.

Jason kept three men constantly on watch, searching the sky for any sign of the myserae, but the creatures remained steadfastly hidden. If he hadn't seen the damage they did to Sattis, he never would have believed they lived here. How could so many creatures vanish so completely?

As night began to fall, the mountains grew still larger and more intimidating. From the map, Jason knew they were fast approaching the end of the island. They had better find the home of the myserae soon or they would have to retrace their steps.

Suddenly, as he gazed up at the mountains, the *Argo* passed a steep ravine and all the shadows fell into place. He found himself staring up into the brooding eyes of a woman. A jagged outcrop of stone made a nose, and a deep cave formed an open mouth. He recognized the face and gave a shudder—*Hera!* There could be no mistaking her fierce, angry expression.

"Lower the sails!" he cried. "Bring us about! This is it!"

"Where is the face?" Hercules called, rushing over with a spear in his hands.

Silently, Jason pointed.

"Where?" Hercules paused, then let out his breath in a long "Ahhh!" as he, too, spotted it.

Witta joined them. "I feel someone watching from the cave. It is a man . . . Vargas, I think. You must strike quickly, before he has time to prepare."

"I didn't expect to surprise him," Jason said grimly. "Keep watch for the myserae, Hercules. I'll see to the rest of the forces. We strike immediately."

"In the dark?" Hercules frowned. "Wouldn't it be better to wait until dawn?"

"If I'm right, the myserae are in that cave," Jason told him. "Day or night, it won't matter once we're inside."

Hercules rowed half of the Argonauts to the beach. As he sat with his back to the mountain, pulling the oars, he felt a strange, unpleasant tingling on the back of his neck. Someone was watching him, he thought . . . someone, or some *thing*.

He put all his effort into the work, and they slid rapidly through the waves. Soon he felt the bottom of the boat scrape sand and knew they had arrived. As several of the men leaped out to pull them ashore, he put the oars away and stood, shouldering the two spears he had brought.

This mountain seemed strangely foreboding: the few scraggly trees on its flanks bore twisted, gnarled trunks and sickly looking yellow leaves. Even the tufts of grass along the edge of the beach had an unhealthy yellowish-brown color. Only thistle seemed to thrive.

He hopped out into ankle-deep surf and waded ashore. The other boat from the *Argo* arrived, and Atalanta greeted him with a grin.

Then they joined Jason and Theseus for a quick war council.

"How will we attack?" Hercules asked. "It's a long way up, and I don't see much of a road."

"This whole place reeks of foul magic," said Witta, eyes narrowing as she stared up at the cave far overhead. "I can see a path in the ravine. That is the way we must go."

"Is there another way?" Jason demanded. "If we go up the ravine, they'll see us and be waiting. Maybe we should find our own way up."

"No," Witta said. "Speed is more important than secrecy, and that will be the quickest route. We must take it."

Jason nodded, hefted his sword and started ahead. Hercules had no intention of being left at the rear, so he jogged forward to catch up, and Atalanta joined them.

The ravine did indeed conceal a path, he found. It twisted and turned, following the natural contours of the land, and at each difficult point, steps had been cut into the rock. It had been built long, long ago; in places, feet had worn the steps until they were almost polished, and the marks of chisels and hammers could barely be seen.

They walked in silence for over an hour. Of the myserae, Hercules saw no sign, but he felt certain they were there, watching, waiting with their master.

Finally they reached a wide terrace halfway to the peak. When Hercules glanced behind him, he saw that half of the men were huffing and out of breath.

"We might want to rest here," he suggested.

"Agreed," Jason said. He sagged down, his back to a large slab of rock, and pulled out a small flagon of wine. After taking a deep swallow, he passed it around. Hercules discovered it was one of Muros's summer wines.

The other Argonauts gathered around and drew water and food from their packs, which they shared between themselves. Jason took a deep swallow from a waterskin, then rose and went to join Witta.

The priestess seemed unbothered by the climb, which Jason found odd, especially considering her age. He'd thought himself in the best of condition, but the muscles in his legs had already begun to ache. He found himself as thankful for the break as were his men.

Hercules joined the two of them, and then Witta walked over and closely examined the slab of stone against which Jason had been resting.

"Is something wrong?" Hercules asked.

"This stone . . . do you think you can move it?"

Hercules regarded it doubtfully. It was taller than he was, and three times as wide. It had to weigh thousands of pounds.

"I can try," he said. "Why?"

"It covers a way into their lair, I think."

Hercules moved to the slab and pressed himself flat against the mountainside. As he did, he noticed a dark space behind the stone and felt a cool breeze blowing gently from behind it. Surely, the slab hid an entrance to a cave.

Jason had been listening, and he hurried to join Hercules in examining the opening.

"Maybe we can all help move it," he suggested.

"Stand back!" Hercules said.

He looked the stone over once, then hooked his fingers around its edge. Setting his feet, he began to pull. Muscles corded in his neck and back; tendons stood out in his arms. He pulled until he thought his fingers would break, and then he pulled harder.

Finally the slab began to move, sliding to one side with a grinding noise. Then it stuck halfway open, and not even his immense strength could budge it another inch. Still, it left a hole large enough for a man to slip through.

Panting, he stepped back. "That's the best I can do," he said.

Witta pushed past him, slipping inside. "Yes," she said, her voice echoing strangely, "this is the way. It's a tunnel."

Jason hefted his sword. "Break out the torches," he said to his men. Hylas and Apeloneus opened their packs and drew them out. Using flint, they struck sparks onto small bundles of kindling until they had a tiny fire, then lit the torches and began passing them out. There were ten in all.

Grabbing one, Jason ducked into the tunnel after Witta. Hercules picked up his spears and followed, then came Atalanta, then the others.

It took a few seconds for Hercules' eyes to adjust to the dimness inside. Witta held her wand up, and it glowed with a cool white light that reminded him of the moon.

"Where will they be?" Jason asked. "And how will you find Vargas?"

"They are all around us, in the nearby passages. I feel a great number of them ahead, massing for an attack. I will take care of them when the time comes. Vargas is our main concern right now. You must help take the pendant from his neck, for that is what he uses to control the creatures. Now, follow me."

Turning, she marched forward.

Before they had gone fifty paces, the tunnel turned and

doubled back, then turned again, joining another, larger passage. This one had small bits of glowing crystal embedded in the walls every few feet. Witta hesitated for a second, looking first one way, then the other, before picking the left branch. Its floor sloped ever so slightly downward, heading deeper into the mountain.

Hearing noises ahead, Jason tensed. He motioned to everyone behind him, and they readied their weapons.

Moving slowly and cautiously, they rounded a corner and entered an immense cavern whose ceiling was lost in flickering shadows. Dozens of passages converged here. Some had been carved out of the limestone; they had huge squared-off openings. Others were simply cave passages.

Hercules sensed movement in the darkness overhead.

"It's an ambush!" he shouted, suddenly realizing the truth. "Get back!"

Jason and the other Argonauts scrambled for the tunnel through which they'd entered, but the air suddenly filled with myserae. They swooped from the ceiling like bats. Others darted in from the passageways all around them. There were hundreds of them, Hercules realized with growing horror.

TWENTY-SIX

JASON GLANCED BACK AND SAW WITTA pressing forward toward the center of the room. She held her wand overhead, and it shone with a clear blue light. The myserae seemed to fear that light, for they shied away from it.

Arrows dropped the first three myserae in the tunnel, but those behind pushed their way inexorably forward. His men would never get out that way, Jason saw.

"Move to the center of the room!" he shouted. Witta was up to something there—

As everyone turned and ran past him, Jason remembered that the creatures feared fire. He called instructions to his men, and they formed a protective ring around Witta, torches outstretched.

The myserae were closing in—

Witta was working her magic, her wand raised toward the roof of the cavern, chanting an invocation to Athena—

Jason found his mouth suddenly dry. They would just

have to hold off the myserae until Witta's magic was done, he thought. Raising his sword, he struck at a myserae darting overhead and sliced through one of its clawed feet. Screaming, the creature flapped away from him. Wielding his torch in his other hand, he thrust it at a second creature, which hissed and banked to the right.

That gave him a free moment. Glancing around to see if anyone needed help, he found Hercules grinning happily, brandishing his spear against two myserae. This was the sort of fight Hercules liked, Jason thought: a test of personal strength against odds that would make the most hardened gambler cringe.

Then suddenly the myserae stopped their attacks. Landing, they formed a circle around the Argonauts. Their heads bobbed left and right; they opened their beaks and hissed. Several paced back and forth, not quite willing to approach the torches. One hopped closer, then another, then a third. They seemed to be working up to an attack. They began chirping wildly among themselves.

Jason glanced back to see how Witta was doing just as she finished her magic. Suddenly the cavern crackled with energy, and blue flames thirty feet high roared up around the circle of men.

Jason pressed his eyes closed, dazed. Bright afterimages like those from looking at the sun too long swam in front of him. Squinting, he tried to focus.

The fire had forced the myserae back, he noticed. The creatures swarmed over one another thirty feet away, unable or unwilling to approach the wall of blue flames. They made little chirping, whistling sounds.

"This way, come quickly!" Witta called.

Jason obeyed. The fire arched overhead now, enclosing them in a tunnel. His men followed as he ran its length, toward the far wall and the dark entrance to another passageway.

He stopped and counted the men as they passed. All were there, and none had taken any serious wounds. Atalanta and Hercules came after them, and then Witta.

The priestess was slowly backing down the passage. She seemed to be directing the blue flames with her wand, shaping them, slowly pulling them back as she retreated.

Suddenly Jason realized what the priestess was doing: she was leading all of the myserae into the cavern, then slowly encircling them with the flames, like a fisherman netting fish. In minutes, she would have all the myserae penned in the middle, walled in with that strange blue fire.

"At last!" Witta cried. "The myserae are trapped. Now we must find Vargas!"

"Where will he be?" Jason demanded.

"Down in the center of the mountain, laying his plans. You and Hercules must help me."

"What of my men?"

"They must stay here to guard the myserae. If my magic fails, none of the creatures must escape!"

Witta led Jason and Hercules through tunnel after tunnel, deeper into the mountain, for what seemed hours. The air grew damp and cold, and in places, water pooled across the floor. Finally they came to a second cavern, this one even higher and wider than the one in which Witta had penned the myserae. Weird flows of rock glistened wetly on the ceiling and walls.

Here, too, were the signs of men: broad steps had been cut into the rock, leading down. The three of them descended farther and farther into the mountain. The passages grew narrow and the ceilings grew low, until both Jason and Hercules had to stoop to continue.

Still, Witta urged them on. "The pendant lies just ahead," she promised.

At last the corridor leveled and opened onto a huge cavern. Against the far wall, raised up on a dais, sat an immense stone throne. Myserae carved from black obsidian formed its sides and back, their eyes glittering red with rubies.

And on the chair sat Vargas.

The chamberlain stood suddenly. The pendant around his neck blazed with a brilliant red light.

"Give it to me," Witta said, holding out her hand, "and we will spare your life."

The chamberlain laughed, but it was with the voice of a woman. "I have been waiting to kill you for a long time. *All* of you."

"If I must, I will take it."

Hercules motioned to Jason, who nodded. Slowly they drifted away from Witta, Jason to the right, Hercules to the left. It was an old strategy: divide your opponent's attention, then strike. The chamberlain didn't seem to be paying the slightest bit of attention to them—which had to mean, Hercules thought uneasily, that Vargas assumed they posed no threat. He remembered Atalanta shooting the chamberlain in Sattis. An arrow through the heart hadn't slowed him down for more than a second.

Sensing a change in the air, Hercules glanced back at Witta. A swirl of golden sparks surrounded her, and as she strode forward, she seemed to grow with every step, her face changing, her body changing. No longer an old woman, she became a proud-faced warrior now, young, armored in silver, with a sword as bright as the sun in her hand.

Vargas, too, moved forward, one hand touching the pendant at his throat. His body twisted, shimmering, and a white myserae loomed there in his place, the pendant around its neck. Beak snapping, it leaped at Witta.

But in a blur of motion, she was gone, dancing to one side, cutting with her sword. Its blade pierced the myserae's left side, and a white liquid bubbled out.

With a roar, the creature rounded on Witta, clawed feet striking. Witta parried, parried again, and yet again as the myserae forced her back step by step.

Hercules continued to watch the fight with awe bordering on amazement. He was half god himself, and as he stared at them, he seemed to see two images laid over one another.

Witta still stood there, but over her, wreathed in blue, was Athena herself, a flaming sword in one hand. Facing her was Vargas, but over him Hercules saw one of Hera's foul creatures.

Hercules' hatred for Hera grew with each passing moment. She had tried again and again to kill him, to wreck his life and ruin his friends. As often as not, she hurt those he cared for.

Jason seemed to be frozen in place, a look of horror on his face. This was more than a mortal was ever meant to see, Hercules realized. Jason would be lucky to survive with his mind intact.

That left only him. With a roar, he drew back his arm and threw his spear with all his strength.

It flew straight, and exactly as he'd meant, it struck the white myserae's head. Unfortunately, it glanced off. But instead of striking the ground, it flew in a circle and struck the pendant hanging around the creature's neck.

The chain snapped; the pendant started to drop. Screeching, the myserae tried to grab it with its beak— and instead, batted it across the room. The pendant skittered to a stop at Hercules' feet.

When Hercules scooped it up, the white myserae shimmered like a reflection in a pond. Howling with anger, it shrank, writhing like a worm cut in two. Suddenly Vargas crouched there, a bent-shouldered old man in a plain white tunic. He gazed up at Witta with an expression of disdain.

"This is not over yet!" he proclaimed in the voice of Hera, the Queen of the Gods.

Witta stalked toward him, a thirty-foot-tall giantess in shining armor.

"Yes it is," Witta said. She brandished her sword.

Vargas screamed and raised his arms.

And Witta clove him in two.

* * *

As Vargas died, Jason seemed to wake as if from a dream. He felt light-headed and confused. Hercules was bending over him, and Witta stalked through the chamber laughing with a young woman's voice.

Things didn't seem to make much sense after that. Later, Jason vaguely recalled scattered images, bright lights, strange colors that seemed to burst from Vargas's body.

He remembered Witta, human-sized once more, but still in her glowing armor, still young and unbelievably beautiful, taking the pendant and putting it around her own neck. The chain was whole—hadn't it been broken? But that didn't seem to matter anymore.

He remembered Hercules picking him up and carrying him down a long passageway that seemed to never end, and he remembered thinking, *This cannot be real.*

"Do not fear," the beautiful woman who had been Witta told him, smiling as she stroked his cheeks and forehead. "I have always looked after you, Jason. I will watch your quest for the Golden Fleece, and I will help you as much as I can."

"Thank you," he whispered.

She smiled, and the beautiful face—the face he suddenly recognized as belonging to Athena—faded, leaving Witta old and wrinkled once more. She clutched the pendant as though drawing strength from it.

"Now," she said in her old voice, "we must take care of the myserae. No more will they plague my people!"

Sometime later, they were back in the huge chamber where the myserae had attacked. Hundreds of the creatures swarmed like bees in the center of the cavern, penned by a circle of blue flames.

Witta grasped the pendant, pointed at the myserae and shouted, "Get back! Get back, foul creatures!"

Instantly they obeyed, climbing over each other, crushing and clawing in their haste to get away. Dozens of them died and hundreds were injured as they formed a huge writhing knot against the far wall of the cavern.

"Stay there!" Witta ordered. She began to back away. The rest of the Argonauts followed, and Hercules pulled Jason along.

Later still, Jason found himself outside, again without transition. He and Hercules and Witta stood near the peak of the myserae's mountain. His breath misted the air. Gazing down, he could see the *Argo* far below, small as a toy on a pond. A line of men—his Argonauts—were just leaving the ravine and hurrying onto the beach.

Witta held the pendant before her. It glowed as hot and white as the sun at noon.

"Now!" she called to Hercules.

Hercules moved to the left, to a huge boulder. Without pause, he set his shoulder against the stone and began to push.

The rock teetered, then slowly toppled, and as it tumbled down the mountainside, it started an avalanche. Tons of rock shifted, sliding down into the ravine. The ground underfoot shook, then grew still.

As dust began to settle, Jason moved to the edge of a new cliff.

The face in the mountain was gone. Both the cave and the tunnel Witta had discovered had been sealed, trapping the myserae inside forever.

"Justice," Witta whispered, "is done."

EPILOGUE

JASON FELT A LIGHT HAND ON HIS shoulder. Turning, he found that Witta had joined him by the rail on board the *Argo*. He still didn't know how they had gotten down off the mountain, but he assumed magic had been involved. With a great rushing wind, they had suddenly been on the deck, waiting impatiently while the rest of his men rowed out to join them.

After that, they had set course for Thorna, and he knew they would reach the island sometime tomorrow afternoon.

"I want to thank you for all you have done," Witta said softly. "It was a brave and courageous thing, to face the myserae."

"It was our duty," he told her. "We could not leave your people suffering, Witta."

"You went beyond duty." She hesitated, then went on: "When I became an instrument for Athena, when she filled my body with her being, I sensed a deep affection for you. You have made an enemy of Hera, but I think you have found an ally in my goddess.''

Jason nodded gravely. ''I know.'' He remembered the touch of her hand on his cheek. He remembered the way she had looked at him. He would make an offering to her temple in every port, he vowed. And he would never forget what she had done to save Witta and her people.

As the *Argo* slipped through the waves, Hercules lay on deck, fingers laced behind his head. He felt thoroughly content as he stared up at the stars.

It had been an exciting adventure, fighting both King Muros and the myserae, and he had to admit that defeating Hera's servants left him deeply satisfied. He chuckled. It felt good for once to have the better of her.

Even so, he knew it was time to return to the task at hand. They had a quest of their own . . . for Jason had still to win the Golden Fleece and his throne.

HERCULES
will return in
The Gates of Hades,
an all-new adventure,
in December, 1997.
Watch for it wherever
Tor Books are sold!

About the author

John Gregory Betancourt has published more than twenty books, including several best-selling Star Trek™ novels and game books for TSR, Inc. You can read more about him and his work at his Internet site— http://www.wildsidepress.com—on the World Wide Web.

TOR
BOOKS The Best in Fantasy

TOR
BOOKS The Best in Fantasy

LORD OF CHAOS • Robert Jordan
Book Six of *The Wheel of Time*. "For those who like to keep themselves in a fantasy world, it's hard to beat the complex, detailed world created here....A great read."—*Locus*

STONE OF TEARS • Terry Goodkind
The sequel to the epic fantasy bestseller *Wizard's First Rule*.

SPEAR OF HEAVEN • Judith Tarr
"The kind of accomplished fantasy—featuring sound characterization, superior world-building, and more than competent prose—that has won Tarr a large audience."—*Booklist*

MEMORY AND DREAM • Charles de Lint
A major novel of art, magic, and transformation, by the modern master of urban fantasy.

NEVERNEVER • Will Shetterly
The sequel to *Elsewhere*. "With a single book, Will Shetterly has redrawn the boundaries of young adult fantasy. This is a remarkable work."—*Bruce Coville*

TALES FROM THE GREAT TURTLE • Edited by Piers Anthony and Richard Gilliam
"A tribute to the wealth of pre-Columbian history and lore."—*Library Journal*